Born in 1906, Fredric Brown was an American science fiction and mystery writer. In early life he attended the University of Cincinnati and Hanover College, Indiana, before working as a newspaperman and magazine writer in the Midwest. His first foray into the mystery genre was *The Fabulous Clipjoint* (1947), which won the Edgar Award from the Mystery Writers of America for outstanding first mystery novel. As an author he wrote more than thirty novels and over three hundred short stories, and is noted for a bold use of narrative experimentation, as exemplified in *The Lenient Beast* (1956). Many of his books employ the threat of the supernatural or occult before concluding with a logical explanation, and he is renowned for both original plots and ingenious endings. In the 1950s he moved to Tucson, Arizona, and wrote for television and film, continuing to submit many short stories that regularly appeared in mystery anthologies. A cultured man and omnivorous reader, Brown had a lifelong interest in the flute, chess, poker, and the works of Lewis Carroll. He died in 1972.

NIGHT OF THE JABBERWOCK

FREDRIC BROWN

THE LANGTAIL PRESS
LONDON

This edition published 2010 by
The Langtail Press

www.langtailpress.com

ISBN 978-1-78002-000-6

NIGHT OF THE
JABBERWOCK

CHAPTER ONE

'Twas brillig, and the slithy toves
Did gyre and gimble in the wabe:
All mimsy were the borogoves,
And the mome raths outgrabe.

IN my dream I was standing in the middle of Oak Street and it was dark night. The streetlights were off; only pale moonlight glinted on the huge sword that I swung in circles about my head as the Jabberwock crept closer. It bellied along the pavement, flexing its wings and tensing its muscles for the final rush; its claws clicked against the stones like the clicking of mats down the channels of a Linotype. Then, astonishingly, it spoke.

"Doc," it said. "Wake up, Doc."

A hand—not the hand of a Jabberwock—was shaking my shoulder.

And it was early dusk instead of black night and I was sitting in the swivel chair at my battered desk, looking over my shoulder at Pete. Pete was grinning at me.

"We're in, Doc," he said. "You'll have to cut two lines on this last take and we're in. Early, for once."

He put a galley proof down in front of me, only one stick of type long. I picked up a blue pencil and knocked off two lines and they happened to be an even sentence, so Pete wouldn't have to reset anything.

He went over to the Linotype and shut it off and it was suddenly very quiet in the place, so quiet that I could hear the drip of the faucet way in the far corner.

I stood up and stretched, feeling good, although a little groggy from having dozed off while Pete was setting that final take. For once, for one Thursday, the *Carmel City Clarion* was ready for the press early. Of course, there wasn't any real news in it, but then there never was.

And only half-past six and not yet dark outside. We were through hours earlier than usual. I decided that that called for a drink, here and now.

The bottle in my desk turned out to have enough whisky in it for one healthy drink or two short ones. I asked Pete if he wanted a snort and he said no, not yet, he'd wait till he got over to Smiley's, so I treated myself to a healthy drink, as I'd hoped to be able to do. And it had been fairly safe to ask Pete; he seldom took one before he was through for the day, and although my part of the job was done Pete still had almost an hour's work ahead of him on the mechanical end.

The drink made a warm spot under my belt as I walked over to the window by the Linotype and stood staring out into the quiet dusk. The lights of Oak Street flashed on while I stood there. I'd been dreaming—what had I been dreaming?

On the sidewalk across the street Miles Harrison hesitated in front of Smiley's Tavern as though the thought of a cool glass of beer tempted him. I could almost feel his mind working: "No, I'm a deputy sheriff of Carmel County and I have a job to do yet tonight and I don't drink while I'm on duty. The beer can wait."

Yes, his conscience must have won, because he walked on.

I wonder now—although of course I didn't wonder then—whether, if he had known that he would be dead before midnight, he wouldn't have stopped for that beer. I think he would have. I know I would have, but that doesn't prove anything because I'd have done it anyway; I've never had a conscience like Miles Harrison's.

Behind me, at the stone, Pete was putting the final stick of type into the chase of the front page. He said, "Okay, Doc, she fits. We're in."

"Let the presses roll," I told him.

Just a manner of speaking, of course. There was only one press and it didn't roll, because it was a Miehle vertical that shuttled up and down. And it wouldn't even do that until morning. The *Clarion* is a weekly paper that comes out on Friday; we put it to bed on Thursday evening and Pete runs it off the press Friday morning. And it's not much of a run.

Pete asked, "You going over to Smiley's?"

That was a silly question; I always go over to Smiley's on a Thursday evening and usually, when he's finished locking up the forms, Pete joins me, at least for a while. "Sure," I told him.

"I'll bring you a stone proof, then," Pete said.

Pete always does that, too, although I seldom do more than glance at it. Pete's too good a printer for me ever to catch any important errors on him and as for minor typographicals, Carmel City doesn't mind them.

I was free and Smiley's was waiting, but for some reason I wasn't in any hurry to leave. It was pleasant, after the hard work of a Thursday— and don't let that short nap fool you; I *had* been working—to stand there and watch the quiet street in the quiet twilight, and to contemplate an intensive campaign of doing nothing for the rest of the evening, with a few drinks to help me do it.

Miles Harrison, a dozen paces past Smiley's, stopped, turned, and headed back. Good, I thought, I'll have someone to drink with. I turned away from the window and put on my suit coat and hat.

I said, "Be seeing you, Pete," and I went down the stairs and out into the warm summer evening.

I'd misjudged Miles Harrison; he was coming out of Smiley's already, too soon even to have had a quick one, and he was opening a pack of cigarettes. He saw me and waved, waiting in front of Smiley's door to light a cigarette while I crossed the street.

"Have a drink with me, Miles," I suggested.

He shook his head regretfully. "Wish I could, Doc. But I got a job to do later. You know, go with Ralph Bonney over to Neilsville to get his pay roll."

Sure, I knew. In a small town everybody knows everything.

Ralph Bonney owned the Bonney Fireworks Company, just outside of Carmel City. They made fireworks, mostly big pieces for fairs and municipal displays, that were sold all over the country. And during the few months of each year up to about the first of July they worked a day and a night shift to meet the Fourth of July demand.

And Ralph Bonney had something against Clyde Andrews, president of the Carmel City Bank, and did his banking in Neilsville. He drove over to Neilsville late every Thursday night and they opened the bank there to give him the cash for his night shift pay roll. Miles Harrison, as deputy sheriff, always went along as guard.

Always seemed like a silly procedure to me, as the night side pay roll didn't amount to more than a few thousand dollars and Bonney could

3

have got it along with the cash for his day side pay roll and held it at the office, but that was his way of doing things.

I said, "Sure, Miles, but that's not for hours yet. And one drink isn't going to hurt you."

He grinned. "I know it wouldn't, but I'd probably take another just because the first one didn't hurt me. So I stick to the rule that I don't have even one drink till I'm off duty for the day, and if I don't stick to it I'm sunk. But thanks just the same, Doc, I'll take a rain check."

He had a point, but I wish he hadn't made it. I wish he'd let me buy him that drink, or several of them, because that rain check wasn't worth the imaginary paper it was printed on to a man who was going to be murdered before midnight.

But I didn't know that, and I didn't insist. I said, "Sure Miles," and asked him about his kids.

"Fine, both of 'em. Drop out and see us sometime."

"Sure," I said, and I went into Smiley's.

Big, bald Smiley Wheeler was alone. He smiled as I came in and said, "Hi, Doc. How's the editing business?" And then he laughed as though he'd said something excruciatingly funny. Smiley hasn't the ghost of a sense of humour and he has the mistaken idea that he disguises that fact by laughing at almost everything he says or hears said.

"Smiley, you give me a pain," I told him. It's always safe to tell Smiley a truth like that; no matter how seriously you say you mean it, he thinks you're joking. If he'd laughed I'd have told him where he gave me a pain, but for once he didn't laugh.

He said, "Glad you got here early, Doc. It's damn dull this evening."

"It's dull every evening in Carmel City," I told him. "And most of the time I like it. But Lord, if only something would happen just once on a Thursday evening, I'd love it. Just once in my long career, I'd like to have *one* hot story to break to a panting public."

"Hell, Doc, nobody looks for hot news in a country weekly."

"I know," I said. "That's why I'd like to fool them just once. I've been running the *Clarion* twenty-three years. One hot story. Is that much to ask?"

Smiley frowned. "There've been a couple of burglaries. And one murder, a few years ago."

4

"Sure," I said, "and so what? One of the factory hands out at Bonney's got in a drunken argument with another and hit him too hard in the fight they got into. That's not murder; that's manslaughter, and anyway it happened on a Saturday and it was old stuff—everybody in town knew about it—by the next Friday when the *Clarion* came out."

"They buy your paper, anyway, Doc. They look for their names for having attended church socials and who's got a used washing machine for sale and—want a drink?"

"It's about time one of us thought of that," I said.

He poured a shot for me and, so I wouldn't have to drink alone, a short one for himself. We drank them and I asked him, "Think Carl will be in tonight?"

I meant Carl Trenholm, the lawyer, who's about my closest friend in Carmel City, and one of the three or four in town who play chess and can be drawn into an intelligent discussion of something beside crops and politics. Carl often dropped in Smiley's on Thursday evenings, knowing that I always came in for at least a few drinks after putting the paper to bed.

"Don't think so," Smiley said. "Carl was in most of the afternoon and got himself kind of a snootful, to celebrate. He got through in court early and he won his case. Guess he went home to sleep it off."

I said, "Damn. Why couldn't he have waited till this evening? I'd have helped him—Say, Smiley, did you say Carl was celebrating because he *won* that case? Unless we're talking about two different things, he lost it. You mean the Bonney divorce?"

"Yeah."

"Then Carl was representing Ralph Bonney, and Bonney's wife won the divorce."

"You got it that way in the paper, Doc?"

"Sure," I said. "It's the nearest thing I've got to a good story this week."

Smiley shook his head. "Carl was saying to me he hoped you wouldn't put it in, or anyway that you'd hold it down to a short squib, just the fact that she got the divorce."

I said, "I don't get it, Smiley. Why? And *didn't* Carl lose the case?"

Smiley leaned forward confidentially across the bar, although he and I were the only ones in his place. He said, "It's like this, Doc. Bonney

5

wanted the divorce. That wife of his was a bitch, see? Only he didn't have any grounds to sue on, himself—not any that he'd have been willing to bring up in court, anyway, see? So he—well, kind of bought his freedom. Gave her a settlement if she'd do the suing, and he admitted to the grounds she gave against him. Where'd you get your version of the story?"

"From the judge," I said.

"Well, he just saw the outside of it. Carl says Bonney's a good joe and those cruelty charges were a bunch of hokum. He never laid a hand on her. But the woman was such hell on wheels that Bonney'd have admitted to anything to get free of her. And give her a settlement of a hundred grand on top of it. Carl was worried about the case because the cruelty charges were so damn silly on the face of them."

"Hell," I said, "that's not the way it's going to sound in the *Clarion*."

"Carl was saying he knew you couldn't tell the truth about the story, but he hoped you'd play it down. Just saying Mrs. B. had been granted a divorce and that a settlement had been made, and not putting in anything about the charges."

I thought of my one real story of the week, and how carefully I'd enumerated all those charges Bonney's wife had made against him, and I groaned at the thought of having to rewrite or cut the story. And cut it I'd have to, now that I knew the facts.

I said, "Damn Carl, why didn't he come and tell *me* about it before I wrote the story and put the paper to bed?"

"He thought about doing that, Doc. And then he decided he didn't want to use his friendship with you to influence the way you reported news."

"The damn fool," I said. "And all he had to do was walk across the street."

"But Carl did say that Bonney's a swell guy and it would be a bad break for him if you listed those charges because none of them were really true and——"

"Don't rub it in," I interrupted him. "I'll change the story. If Carl says it's that way, I'll believe him. I can't say that the charges weren't true, but at least I can leave them out."

"That'd be swell of you, Doc."

"Sure it would. All right, give me one more drink, Smiley, and I'll go over and catch it before Pete leaves."

I had the one more drink, cussing myself for being sap enough to spoil the only mentionable story I had, but knowing I had to do it. I didn't know Bonney personally, except just to say hello to on the street, but I did know Carl Trenholm well enough to be damn sure that if he said Bonney was in the right, the story wasn't fair the way I'd written it. And I knew Smiley well enough to be sure he hadn't given me a bum steer on what Carl had really said.

So I grumbled my way back across the street and upstairs to the *Clarion* office. Pete was just tightening the chase around the front page.

He loosened the quoins when I told him what we had to do, and I walked around the stone so I could read the story again, upside down of course, as type is always read.

The first paragraph could stand as written and could constitute the entire story. I told Pete to put the rest of the type in the hellbox and I went over to the case and set a short head in tenpoint, *"Bonney Divorce Granted,"* to replace the twenty-four-point head that had been on the longer story. I handed Pete the stick and watched while he switched heads.

"Leaves about a nine-inch hole in the page," he said. "What'll we stick in it?"

I sighed. "Have to use filler," I told him. "Not on the front page, but we'll have to find something on page four we can move front and then stick in nine inches of filler where it came from."

I wandered down the stone to page four and picked up a pica stick to measure things. Pete went over to the rack and got a galley of filler. About the only thing that was anywhere near the right size was the story that Clyde Andrews, Carmel's City's banker and leading light of the local Baptist Church, had given me about the rummage sale the church had planned for next Tuesday evening.

It wasn't exactly a story of earth-shaking importance, but it would be about the right length if we reset it indented to go in a box. And it had a lot of names in it, and that meant it would please a lot of people, and particularly Clyde Andrews, if I moved it up to the front page.

So we moved it. Rather, Pete reset it for a front page box item while I plugged the gap in page four with filler items and locked up the page again. Pete had the rummage sale item reset by the time I'd finished with page four, and this time I waited for him to finish up page one, so we could go to Smiley's together.

I thought about that front page while I washed my hands. *The Front Page*. Shades of Hecht and MacArthur. Poor revolving Horace Greeley.

Now I really wanted a drink.

Pete was starting to pound out a stone proof and I told him not to bother. Maybe the customers would read page one, but I wasn't going to. And if there was an upside-down headline or a pied paragraph, it would probably be an improvement.

Pete washed up and we locked the door. It was still early for a Thursday evening, not much after seven. I should have been happy about that, and I probably would have been if we'd had a good paper. As for the one we'd just put to bed, I wondered if it would live until morning.

Smiley had a couple of other customers and was waiting on them, and I wasn't in any mood to wait for Smiley so I went around behind the bar and got the Old Henderson bottle and two glasses and took them to a table for Pete and myself. Smiley and I know one another well enough so it's always all right for me to help myself any time it's convenient and settle with him afterward.

I poured drinks for Pete and me. We drank and Pete said, "Well, that's that for another week, Doc."

I wondered how many times he'd said that in the ten years he'd worked for me, and then I got to wondering how many times I'd thought it, which would be———

"How much is fifty-two times twenty-three, Pete?" I asked him.

"Huh? A hell of a lot. Why?"

I figured it myself. "Fifty times twenty-three is—one thousand one hundred and fifty; twice twenty-three more makes eleven ninety-six. Peter, eleven hundred and ninety-six times have I put that paper to bed on a Thursday night and never once was there a really *big* hot news story in it."

"This isn't Chicago, Doc. What do you expect, a murder?"

"I'd love a murder," I told him.

It would have been funny if Pete had said, "Doc, how'd you like three in one night?"

8

But he didn't of course. In a way, though, he said something that was even funnier. He said, "But suppose it was a friend of yours? Your best friend, say, Carl Trenholm. Would you want him killed just to give the *Clarion* a story?"

"Of course not," I said. "Preferably somebody I don't know at all—if there *is* anybody in Carmel City I don't know at all. Let's make it Yehudi."

"Who's Yehudi?" Pete asked.

I looked at Pete to see if he was kidding me, and apparently he wasn't, so I explained: "The little man who wasn't there. Don't you remember the rhyme?

> *I saw a man upon the stair,*
> *A little man who was not there.*
> *He was not here again today;*
> *Gee, I wish he'd go away."*

Pete laughed. "Doc, you get crazier every day. Is that *Alice in Wonderland,* too, like all the other stuff you quote when you get drinking?"

"This time, no. But who says I quote Lewis Carroll only when I'm drinking? I can quote him now, and I've hardly started drinking for tonight—why, as the Red Queen said to Alice, 'One has to do *this* much drinking to stay in the same place.' But listen and I'll quote you something that's really something:

> *'Twas brillig and the slithy toves*
> *Did gyre and gimble in the wabe——"*

Pete stood up. "*Jabberwocky,* from *Alice Through the Looking-Glass,*" he said. "If you've recited that to me once, Doc, it's been a hundred times. I damn near know it myself. But I got to go, Doc. Thanks for the drink."

"Okay, Pete, but don't forget one thing."

"What's that?"

I said:

> *"Beware the Jabberwock, my son!*
> *The jaws that bite, the claws that catch!*
> *Beware the Jubjub bird, and shun*
> *The frumious——"*

9

Smiley was calling to me, "Hey, Doc!" from over beside the telephone and I remembered now that I'd heard it ring half a minute before. Smiley yelled, "Telephone for you, Doc," and laughed as though that was the funniest thing that had happened in a long time.

I stood up and started for the phone, telling Pete good night *en route*.

I picked up the phone and said, "Hello" to it and it said "Hello" back to me. Then it said, "Doc?" and I said, "Yes."

Then it said, "Clyde Andrews speaking, Doc." His voice sounded quite calm. "This is murder."

Pete must be almost to the door by now; that was my first thought. I said, "Just a second, Clyde," and then jammed my hand over the mouthpiece while I yelled, "Hey, Pete!"

He *was* at the door, but he turned.

"Don't go," I yelled at him, the length of the bar. "There's a *murder story* breaking. We got to remake!"

I could feel the sudden silence in Smiley's Bar. The conversation between the two other customers stopped in the middle of a word and they turned to look at me. Pete, from the door, looked at me. Smiley, a bottle in his hand, turned to look at me—and he didn't even smile. In fact, just as I turned back to the phone, the bottle dropped out of his hand and hit the floor with a noise that made me jump and close my mouth quickly to keep my heart from jumping from it. That bottle crashing on the floor had sounded—for a second—just like a revolver shot.

I waited until I felt that I could talk again without stammering and then I took my hand off the mouthpiece of the phone and said calmly, or almost calmly, "Okay, Clyde, go ahead."

CHAPTER TWO

"Who are you, aged man?" I said.
"And how is it you live?"
His answer trickled through my head,
Like water through a sieve.

"YOU'VE gone to press, haven't you, Doc?" Clyde's voice said. "You must have because I tried phoning you at the office first and then somebody told me if you weren't there, you'd be at Smiley's, but that'd mean you were through for the———"

"That's all right," I said. "Get on with it."

"I know it's murder, Doc, to ask you to change a story when you've already got the paper ready to run and have left the office, but—well, that rummage sale we were going to have Tuesday; it's been called off. Can you still kill the article? Otherwise a lot of people will read about it and come around to the church Tuesday night and be disappointed."

"Sure, Clyde," I said. "I'll take care of it."

I hung up. I went over to the table and sat down. I poured myself a drink of whisky and when Pete came over I poured him one.

He asked me what the call had been and I told him.

Smiley and his two other customers were still staring at me, but I didn't say anything until Smiley called out, "What happened, Doc? Didn't you say something about a murder?"

I said, "I was just kidding, Smiley." He laughed.

I drank my drink and Pete drank his. He said, "I knew there was a catch about getting through early tonight. Now we got a nine-inch hole in the front page all over again. What are we going to put in it?"

"Damned if I know," I told him. "But the hell with it for tonight. I'll get down when you do in the morning and figure something out then."

Pete said, "That's what you say, now, Doc. But if you *don't* get down at eight o'clock, what'll I do with that hole in the page?"

"Your lack of faith horrifies me, Pete. If I say I'll be down in the morning, I will be. Probably."

"But if you're not?"

I sighed. "Do anything you want." I knew Pete would fix it up somehow if I didn't get down. He'd drag something from a back page and plug the back page with filler items or a subscription ad.

It was going to be lousy because we had one sub ad in already and too damn much filler; you know, those little items that tell you the number of board feet in a sequoia and the current rate of mullet manufacture in the Euphrates valley. All right in small doses, but when you run the stuff by the column——

Pete said he'd better go, and this time he did. I watched him go, envying him a little. Pete Corey is a good printer and I pay him just about what I make myself. We put in about the same number of hours, but I'm the one who has to worry whenever there's any worrying to be done, which is most of the time.

Smiley's other customers left, just after Pete, and I didn't want to sit alone at the table, so I took my bottle over to the bar.

"Smiley," I said, "do you want to buy a paper?"

"Huh?" Then he laughed. "You're kidding me, Doc. It isn't off the press till tomorrow noon is it?"

"It isn't," I told him. "But it'll be well worth waiting for this week. Watch for it, Smiley. But that isn't what I meant."

"Huh? Oh, you mean do I want to buy the *paper*. I don't think so, Doc. I don't think I'd be very good at running a paper. I can't spell very good, for one thing. But look, you were telling me the other night Clyde Andrews wanted to buy it from you. Why'n't you sell it to him, if you want to sell it?"

"Who the devil said I wanted to sell it?" I asked him. "I just asked if you wanted to buy it."

Smiley looked baffled.

"Doc," he said. "I never know whether you're serious or not. Seriously, do you really want to sell out?"

I'd been wondering that. I said slowly, "I don't know, Smiley. Right now, I'd be damn tempted. I think I hate to quit mostly because before I do I'd like to get out one *good* issue. Just one *good* issue out of twenty-three years."

"If you sold it, what'd you do?"

"I guess, Smiley, I'd spend the rest of my life not editing a newspaper."

Smiley decided I was being funny again, and laughed.

The door opened and Al Grainger came in. I waved the bottle at him and he came down the bar to where I was standing, and Smiley got another glass and a chaser of water; Al always needs a chaser.

Al Grainger is just a young squirt—twenty-two or -three—but he's one of the few chess players in town and one of the even fewer people who understands my enthusiasm for Lewis Carroll. Besides that, he's by way of being a Mystery Man in Carmel City. Not that you have to be very mysterious to achieve that distinction.

He said, "Hi, Doc. When are we going to have another game of chess?"

"No time like the present, Al. Here and now?"

Smiley kept chessmen on hand for screwy customers like Al Grainger and Carl Trenholm and myself. He'd bring them out, always handling them as though he expected them to explode in his hands, whenever we asked for them.

Al shook his head. "Wish I had time. Got to go home and do some work."

I poured whisky in his glass and spilled a little trying to fill it to the brim. He shook his head slowly. "The White Knight is sliding down the poker," he said. "He balances very badly."

"I'm only in the second square," I told him. "But the next move will be a good one. I go to the fourth by train, remember."

"Don't keep it waiting, Doc. The smoke alone is worth a thousand pounds a puff."

Smiley was looking from one of us to the other. "What the hell are you guys talking about?" he wanted to know.

13

There wasn't any use trying to explain. I levelled my finger at him. I said, "Crawling at your feet you may observe a bread-and-butter fly. Its wings are thin slices of bread-and-butter, its body a crust and its head is a lump of sugar. And it lives on weak tea with cream in it."

Al said, "Smiley, you're supposed to ask him what happens if it can't find any."

I said, "Then I say it would die of course and you say that must happen very often and I say it *always* happens."

Smiley looked at us again and shook his head slowly. He said, "You guys are *really* nuts." He walked down the bar to wash and wipe some glasses.

Al Grainger grinned at me. "What are your plans for tonight, Doc?" he asked. "I just might possibly be able to sneak in a game or two of chess later. You going to be home, and up?"

I nodded. "I was just working myself up to the idea of walking home, and when I get there I'm going to read. And have another drink or two. If you get there before midnight I'll still be sober enough to play. Sober enough to beat a young punk like you, anyway."

It was all right to say that last part because it was so obviously untrue. Al had been beating me two games out of three for the last year or so.

He chuckled, and quoted at me:

> " 'You are old, Father William,' the young man said,
> 'And your hair has become very white;
> And yet you incessantly stand on your head—
> Do you think, at your age, it is right?' "

Well, since Carroll had the answer to that, so did I:

> " 'In my youth,' Father William replied to his son,
> I feared it might injure the brain;
> But now that I'm perfectly sure I have none,
> Why, I do it again and again.' "

Al said, "Maybe you got something there, Doc. But let's quit alternating verses on that before you get to 'Be off, or I'll kick you down-stairs!' Because I got to be off anyway."

"One more drink?"

"I – think not, not till I'm through working. You can drink and think too. Hope I can do the same thing when I'm your age. I'll try my best to get to your place for some chess, but don't look for me unless I'm there by ten o'clock—half past at the latest. And thanks for the drink."

He went out and, through Smiley's window, I could see him getting into his shiny convertible. He blew the Klaxon and waved back at me as he pulled out from the kerb.

I looked at myself in the mirror back of Smiley's bar and wondered how old Al Grainger thought I was. *"Hope I can do the same thing when I'm your age,"* indeed. Sounded as though he thought I was eighty, at least. I'll be fifty-three my next birthday.

But I had to admit that I looked that old, and that my hair was turning white. I watched myself in the mirror and that whiteness scared me just a little. No, I wasn't old yet, but I was getting that way. And, much as I crab about it, I like living. I don't want to get old and I don't want to die. Especially as I can't look forward, as a good many of my fellow townsmen do, to an eternity of harp playing and picking bird-lice out of my wings. Nor, for that matter, an eternity of shovelling coal, although that would probably be the more likely of the two in my case.

Smiley came back. He jerked his finger at the door. "I don't like that guy, Doc," he said.

"Al? He's all right. A little wet behind the ears, maybe. You're just prejudiced because you don't know where his money comes from. Maybe he's got a printing press and makes it himself. Come to think of it, *I've* got a printing press. Maybe I should try that myself."

"Hell, it ain't that, Doc. It's not my business how a guy earns his money—or where he gets it if he don't earn it. It's the way he talks. *You* talk crazy, too, but—well, you do it in a nice way. When he says something to me I don't understand he says it in a way that makes me feel like a stupid bastard. Maybe I *am* one, but——"

I felt suddenly ashamed of all the things I'd ever said to Smiley that I knew he wouldn't understand.

I said, "It's not a matter of intelligence, Smiley. It's merely a matter of literary background. Have one drink with me, and then I'd better go."

I poured him a drink and—this time—a small one for myself. I was beginning to feel the effects, and I didn't want to get too drunk to give Al Grainger a good game of chess if he dropped in.

I said, for no reason at all, "You're a good guy, Smiley," and he laughed and said, "So are you, Doc. Literary background or not, you're a little crazy, but you're a good guy."

And then, because we were both embarrassed at having caught ourselves saying things like that, I found myself staring past Smiley at the calendar over the bar. It had the usual kind of picture one sees on bar room calendars—an almost too voluptuous naked woman—and it was imprinted by Beal Brothers Store.

It was just a bit of bother to keep the eyes focused on it, I noticed, although I hadn't had enough to drink to affect my mind at all. Right then, for instance, I was thinking of two things at one and the same time. Part of my brain, to my disgust, persisted in wondering if I could get Beal Brothers to start running a quarter page ad instead of an eighth page; I tried to squelch the thought by telling myself that I didn't care, tonight, whether anybody advertised in the *Clarion* at all, and that part of my brain went on to ask me why, damn it, if I felt that way about it, I didn't get out from under while I had the chance by selling the *Clarion* to Clyde Andrews. But the other part of my mind kept getting more and more annoyed by the picture on the calendar, and I said, "Smiley, you ought to take down that calendar. It's a lie. There *aren't* any women like that."

He turned around and looked at it. "Guess you're right. Doc; there aren't any women like that. But a guy can dream, can't he?"

"Smiley," I said, "if that's not the first profound thing you've said, it's the *most* profound. You are right, moreover. You have my full permission to leave the calendar up."

He laughed and moved along the bar to finish wiping glasses, and I stood there and wondered why I didn't go on home. It was still early, a few minutes before eight o'clock. I didn't want another drink, yet. But by the time I got home, I would want one.

So I got out my wallet and called Smiley back. We estimated how many drinks I'd poured out of the bottle and I settled for them, and then I bought another bottle, a full quart, and he wrapped it for me.

I went out with it under my arm and said "So long, Smiley," and he said "So long, Doc," just as casually as though, before the gibbering night that hadn't started yet was over, he and I would not—but let's take things as they happened.

The walk home.

I had to go past the post office anyway, so I stopped in. The mail windows were closed, of course, but the outer lobby is always left open evenings so those who have post office boxes can get mail out of them.

I got my mail—there wasn't anything important in it—and then stopped, as I usually do, by the bulletin board to look over the notices and the wanted circulars that were posted there.

There were a couple of new ones and I read them and I studied the pictures. I've got a good memory for faces, even ones I've just seen pictures of, and I'd always hoped that some day I'd spot a wanted criminal in Carmel City and get a story out of it, if not a reward.

A few doors farther on I passed the bank and that reminded me about its president, Clyde Andrews, and his wanting to buy the paper from me. He didn't want to run it himself, of course; he had a brother somewhere in Ohio who'd had newspaper experience and who would run the paper for Andrews if I sold it to him.

The thing I liked least about the idea, I decided, was that Andrews was in politics and if he controlled the *Clarion*, the *Clarion* would back his party. The way I ran it, it threw mud at both factions when they deserved it, which was often, and handed either one an occasional bouquet when deserved, which was seldom. Maybe I'm crazy—other people than Smiley and Al have said so—but that's the way I think a newspaper should be run, and especially when it's the only paper in a town.

It's not, I might mention, the best way to make money. It had made me plenty of friends and subscribers, but a newspaper doesn't make money from its subscribers. It makes money from advertisers and most of the men in town big enough to be advertisers had fingers in politics and no matter which party I slammed I was likely to lose another advertising account.

I'm afraid that policy didn't help my news coverage, either. The best source of news is the sheriff's department and, at the moment, Sheriff Rance Kates was just about my worst enemy. Kates is honest, but he is also stupid, rude and full of race prejudice; and race prejudice, although it's not a burning issue in Carmel City, is one of my pet peeves. I hadn't pulled any punches in my editorials about Kates, either before or after his election. He got into office only because his opponent—who wasn't any intellectual heavyweight either—had got into a tavern brawl in Neilsville a week before election and was arrested there and charged with assault and battery. The *Clarion* had reported that, too, so the *Clarion* was probably responsible for Rance Kates' being elected sheriff. But Rance remembered only the things I'd said about *him,* and barely spoke to me on the street. Which, I might add, didn't concern me the slightest bit personally, but it forced me to get all of my police news, such as it is, the hard way.

Past the supermarket and Beal Brothers and past Deak's Music Store—where I'd once bought a violin but had forgotten to get a set of instructions with it—and the corner and across the street.

The walk home.

Maybe I weaved just a little, for at just that stage I'm never quite as sober as I am later on. But my mind—ah, it was in that delightful state of being crystal clear in the centre and fuzzy around the edges, the state that every moderate drinker knows but can't explain or define, the state that makes even a Carmel City seem delightful and such things as its squalid politics amusing.

Past the corner drugstore—Pop Hinkle's place—where I used to drink sodas when I was a kid, before I went away to college and made the big mistake of studying journalism. Past Gorham's Feed Store, where I'd worked vacations while I was in high school. Past the Bijou Theatre. Past Hank Greeber's Undertaking Parlours, through which both of my parents had passed, fifteen and twenty years ago.

Around the corner at the courthouse, where a light was still on in Sheriff Kates' office—and I felt so cheerful that, for a thousand dollars or so, I'd have stopped in to talk to him. But no one was around to offer me a thousand dollars.

Out of the store district now, past the house in which Elsie Minton had lived—and in which she had died while we were engaged, twenty-five years ago.

Past the house Elmer Conklin had lived in when I'd bought the *Clarion* from him. Past the church where I'd been sent to Sunday School when I was a kid, and where I'd once won a prize for memorizing verses of the Bible.

Past my past, and walking, slightly weaving, toward the house in which I'd been conceived and born.

No, I hadn't lived there fifty-three years. My parents had sold it and had moved to a bigger house when I was nine and when my sister— now married and living in Florida—had been born. I'd bought it back twelve years ago when it happened to be vacant and on the market at a good price. It's only a three-room cottage, not too big for a man to live in alone, if he likes to live alone, and I do.

Oh, I like people too. I like someone to drop in for conversation or chess or a drink or all three. I like to spend an hour or two in Smiley's, or any other tavern, a few times a week. I like an occasional poker game.

But I'll settle, on any given evening, for my books. Two walls of my living-room are lined with them and they overflow into bookcases in my bedroom and I even have a shelf of them in the bathroom. What do I mean, even? I think a bathroom without a bookshelf is as incomplete as would be one without a toilet.

And they're good books, too. No, I wouldn't be lonely tonight, even if Al Grainger didn't come around for that game of chess. How could I be lonesome with a bottle in my pocket and good company waiting for me? Why, reading a book is almost as good as listening to the man who wrote it talking to you. Better in one way, because you don't have to be polite to him. You can shut him up any moment you feel so inclined and pick someone else instead. And you can take off your shoes and put your feet on the table. You can drink and read until you forget everything but what you're reading; you can forget who you are and the fact that there's a newspaper that hangs around your neck like a millstone, all day and every day, until you get home to sanctuary and forgetfulness.

The walk home.

And so to the corner of Campbell Street and my turning.

A June evening, but cool, and the night air had almost completely sobered me in the nine blocks I'd walked from Smiley's.

My turning, and I saw that the light was on in the front room of my house. I started walking a little faster, mildly puzzled. I knew I hadn't left it on when I'd left for the office that morning. And if I *had* left it on,

Mrs. Carr, the cleaning woman who comes in for about two hours every afternoon to keep my place in order, would have turned it off.

Maybe, I thought, Al Grainger had finished whatever he was doing and had come early and had—but no, Al wouldn't have come without his car and there wasn't any car parked in front.

It might have been a mystery, but it wasn't.

Mrs. Carr was there, putting on her hat in front of the panel mirror in the closet door as I went in.

She said, "I'm just leaving, Mr. Stoeger. I wasn't able to get here this afternoon, so I came to clean up this evening instead; I just finished."

"Fine," I said. "By the way, there's a blizzard out."

"A—what?"

"Blizzard. Snowstorm." I held up the wrapped bottle. "So maybe you'd better have a little nip with me before you start home, don't you think?"

She laughed. "Thanks, Mr. Stoeger. I will. I've had a pretty rough day, and it sounds like a good idea. I'll get glasses for us."

I put my hat in the closet and followed her out into the kitchen.

"A rough day?" I asked her. "I hope nothing went wrong."

"Well—nothing too serious. My husband—he works, you know, out at Bonney's fireworks factory—got burned in a little accident they had out there this afternoon, and they brought him home. It's nothing serious, a second-degree burn the doctor said, but it was pretty painful and I thought I'd better stay with him until after supper, and then he finally got to sleep so I ran over here and I'm afraid I straightened up your place pretty fast and didn't do a very good job."

"Looks spotless to me," I said. I'd been opening the bottle while she'd been getting glasses for us. "I hope he'll be all right, Mrs Carr. But if you want to skip coming here for a while———"

"Oh, no, I can still come. He'll be home only a few days, and it was just that today they brought him home at two o'clock, just when I was getting ready to come here and—That's plenty, thanks."

We touched glasses and I downed mine while she drank about half of hers. She said, "Oh, there was a phone call for you, about an hour ago. A little while after I got here."

"Find out who it was?"

"He wouldn't tell me, just said it wasn't important."

I shook my head sadly. "That, Mrs. Carr, is one of the major fallacies of the human mind. The idea, I mean, that things can be arbitrarily divided into the important and the unimportant. How can anyone decide whether a given fact is important or not unless one knows *everything* about it—and no one knows everything about anything."

She smiled, but a bit vaguely, and I decided to bring it down to earth, I said. "What would you say is important, Mrs. Carr?"

She put her head on one side and considered it seriously. "Well, *work* is important, isn't it?"

"It is not," I told her. "I'm afraid you score zero. Work is only a means to an end. We work in order to enable ourselves to do the important things, which are the things we want to do. Doing what we want to do— that's what's important, if anything is."

"That sounds like a funny way of putting it, but maybe you're right. Well, anyway, this man who called said he'd either call again or come around. I told him you probably wouldn't be home until eight or nine o'clock."

She finished her drink and declined an encore. I walked to the front door with her, saying that I'd have been glad to drive her home but that my car had two flat tyres. I'd discovered them that morning when I'd started to drive to work. One I might have stopped to fix, but two discouraged me; I decided to leave the car in the garage until Saturday afternoon, when I'd have lots of time. And then, too, I know that I *should* get the exercise of walking to and from work every day, but as long as my car is in running condition, I don't. For Mrs. Carr's sake, though, I wished now that I'd fixed the tyres.

She said, "It's only a few blocks, Mr. Stoeger. I wouldn't think of letting you, even if your car was working. Good night."

"Oh, just a minute, Mrs. Carr. What department at Bonney's does your husband work in?"

"The Roman candle department."

It made me forget, for the moment, what I'd been leading up to. I said, "The Roman candle department! That's a wonderful phrase; I love it. If I sell the paper, darned if I don't look up Bonney the very next day. I'd love to work in the Roman candle department. Your husband is a lucky man."

"You're joking, Mr. Stoeger. But are you really thinking of selling the paper?"

"Well—thinking of it." And that reminded me. "I didn't get any story on the accident at Bonney's, didn't even hear about it. And I'm badly in need of a story for the front page. Do you know the details of what happened? Anyone else hurt?"

She'd been part way across the front porch, but she turned and came back nearer the door. She said, "Oh, *please* don't put it in the paper. It wasn't anything important; my husband was the only one hurt and it was his own fault, he said. And Mr. Bonney wouldn't like it being in the paper; he has enough trouble now getting as many people as he needs for the rush season before the Fourth, and so many people are afraid to work around powder and explosives anyway. George will probably be fired if it gets written up in the paper and he *needs* the work."

I sighed; it had been an idea while it lasted. I assured her that I wouldn't print anything about it. And if George Carr had been the only one hurt and I didn't have any details, it wouldn't have made over a one-inch item anyway.

I would have loved, though, to get that beautiful phrase, *"the Roman candle department,"* into print.

I went back inside and closed the door. I made myself comfortable by taking off my suit coat and loosening my tie, and then I got the whisky bottle and my glass and put them on the coffee table in front of the sofa.

I didn't take the tie off yet, nor my shoes; it's nicer to do those things one at a time as you gradually get more and more comfortable.

I picked out a few books and put them within easy reach, poured myself a drink, sat down, and opened one of the books.

The doorbell rang.

Al Grainger had come early, I thought. I went to the door and opened it. There was a man standing there, just lifting his hand to ring again. But it wasn't Al; it was a man I'd never seen before.

CHAPTER THREE

How cheerfully he seems to grin
How neatly spreads his claws,
And welcomes little fishes in
With gently smiling jaws!

HE was short, about my own height, perhaps, but seeming even shorter because of his greater girth. The first thing you noticed about his face was his nose; it was long, thin, pointed, grotesquely at variance with his pudgy body. The light coming past me through the doorway reflected glowing points in his eyes, giving them a catlike gleam. Yet there was nothing sinister about him. A short pudgy man can never manage to seem sinister, no matter how the light strikes his eyes.

"You are Doctor Stoeger?" he asked.

"Doc Stoeger," I corrected him. "But not a doctor of medicine. If you're looking for a medical doctor, one lives four doors west of here."

He smiled, a nice smile. "I am aware that you are not a medico, Doctor, Ph.D., Burgoyne College—nineteen twenty-two, I believe. Author of *Lewis Carroll Through the Looking-Glass* and *Red Queen and White Queen.*"

It startled me. Not so much that he knew my college and the year of my *magna cum laude,* but the rest of it was amazing. *Lewis Carroll Through the Looking-Glass* was a monograph of a dozen pages; it had been printed eighteen years ago and only a hundred copies had been run off. If one still existed anywhere outside of my own library, I was greatly surprised. And *Red Queen and White Queen* was a magazine article that had appeared at least twelve years ago in a magazine that had been obscure then and had long since been discontinued and forgotten.

"Yes," I said. "But how you know of them, I can't imagine, Mr.——"

"Smith," he said gravely. Then he chuckled. "And the first name is Yehudi."

"No!" I said.

"Yes. You see, Doctor Stoeger, I was named forty years ago, when the name Yehudi, although uncommon, had not yet acquired the comic connotation which it has today. My parents did not guess that the name would become a joke—and that it would be particularly ridiculous when combined with Smith. Had they guessed the difficulty I now have in convincing people that I'm not kidding them when I tell them my name——" He laughed ruefully.

"I always carry cards."

He handed me one. It read:

Yehudi Smith

There was no address, no other information. Just the same, I wanted to keep that card, so I stuck it in my pocket instead of handing it back.

He said, "People *are* named Yehudi, you know. There's Yehudi Menuhin, the violinist. And there's——"

"Stop, please," I interrupted. "You're making it plausible. I liked it better the other way."

He smiled. "Then I haven't misjudged you, Doctor. Have you ever heard of the Vorpal Blades?"

"Plural? No. Of course, in Jabberwocky:

One, two! One, two! and through and through
The vorpal blade went snicker-snack!

But—Good God! Why are we talking about vorpal blades through a doorway? Come on in, I've got a bottle, and I hope and presume that it would be ridiculous to ask a man who talks about vorpal blades whether or not he drinks."

I stepped back and he came in. "Sit anywhere," I told him. "I'll get another glass. Want either a mix or a chaser?"

He shook his head, and I went out into the kitchen and got another glass. I came in, filled it and handed it to him. He'd already made himself comfortable in the overstuffed chair.

I sat back on the sofa and lifted my glass toward him. I said, "No doubt about a toast for this one. To Charles Lutwidge Dodgson, known, when in Wonderland, as Lewis Carroll."

He said, quietly, "Are you sure, Doctor?"

"Sure of what?"

"Of your phraseology in that toast. I'd word it: To Lewis Carroll, who masqueraded under the alleged identity of Charles Lutwidge Dodgson, the gentle don of Oxford."

I felt vaguely disappointed. Was this going to be another, and even more ridiculous, Bacon-was-Shakespeare deal? Historically, there couldn't be any possible doubt that the Reverend Dodgson, writing under the name Lewis Carroll, had created *Alice in Wonderland* and its sequel.

But the main point, for the moment, was to get the drink drunk.

So I said solemnly, "To avoid all difficulties, factual or semantic, Mr. Smith, let's drink to the author of the Alice books."

He inclined his head with solemnity equal to my own, then tilted it back and downed his drink. I was a little late in downing mine because of my surprise at, and admiration for, his manner of drinking. I'd never seen anything quite like it. The glass had stopped, quite suddenly, a good three inches from his mouth. And the whisky had kept on going and not a drop of it had been lost. I've seen people toss down a shot before, but never with such casual precision and from so great a distance.

I drank my own in a more prosaic manner, but I resolved to try his system sometime—in private and with a towel or handkerchief ready at hand.

I refilled our glasses and then said, "And now what? Do we argue the identity of Lewis Carroll?"

"Let's start back of that," he said. "In fact, let's put it aside until I can offer you definite proof of what we believe—rather, of what we are certain."

"We?"

"The Vorpal Blades. An organization. A very small organization, I should add."

"Of admirers of Lewis Carroll?"

He leaned forward. "Yes, of course. Any man who is both literate and imaginative is an admirer of Lewis Carroll. But—much more than that. We have a secret. A quite esoteric one."

"Concerning the identity of Lewis Carroll? You mean that you believe—the way some people believe, or used to believe, that the plays of Shakespeare were written by Francis Bacon—that someone other than Charles Lutwidge Dodgson wrote the Alice books?"

I hoped he'd say no.

He said, "No. We believe that Dodgson himself—How much do you know of him, Doctor?"

"He was born in eighteen thirty-two," I said, "and died just before the turn of the century—in either ninety-eight or nine. He was an Oxford don, a mathematician. He wrote several treatises on mathematics. He liked—and created—acrostics and other puzzles and problems. He never married but he was very fond of children, and his best writing was done for them. At least he *thought* he was writing only for children; actually, *Alice in Wonderland* and *Alice Through the Looking-Glass*, while having plenty of appeal for children, are adult literature, and great literature. Shall I go on?"

"By all means."

"He was also capable of—and perpetrated—some almost incredibly bad writing. There ought to be a law against the printing of volumes of *The Complete Works of Lewis Carroll*. He should be remembered for the great things he wrote, and the bad ones interred with his bones. Although I'll admit that even the bad things have occasional touches of brilliance. There are moments in *Sylvie and Bruno* that are almost worth reading through the thousands of dull words to reach. And there are occasional good lines or stanzas in even the worst poems. Take the first three lines of *The Palace of Humbug*:

I dreamt I dwelt in marble halls,
And each damp thing that creeps and crawls
Went wobble-wobble on the walls.

"Of course he should have stopped there instead of adding fifteen or twenty bad triads. But *'Went wobble-wobble on the walls'* is marvellous."

He nodded. "Let's drink to it."

We drank to it.

He said, "Go on."

"No," I said. "I'm just realizing that I could easily go on for hours. I can quote every line of verse in the Alice books and most of *The Hunting of the Snark*. But, I both hope and presume, you didn't come here to listen to me lecture on Lewis Carroll. My information about him is fairly thorough, but quite orthodox. I judge that yours isn't, and I want to hear it."

I refilled our glasses.

He nodded slowly. "Quite right, Doctor. My—I should say *our*—information is extremely unorthodox. I think you have the background and the type of mind to understand it, and to believe it when you have seen proof. To a more ordinary mind, it would seem sheer fantasy."

It was getting better by the minute. I said, "Don't stop now."

"Very well. But before I go any further, I must warn you of something, Doctor. It is also very dangerous information to have. I do not speak lightly or metaphorically. I mean that there is serious danger, deadly danger."

"That," I said, "is wonderful."

He sat there and toyed with his glass—still with the third drink in it—and didn't look at me. I studied his face. It was an interesting face. That long, thin, pointed nose, so incongruous to his build that it might have been false—a veritable Cyrano de Bergerac of a nose. And now that he was in the light, I could see that there were deep laughter-lines around his generous mouth. At first I would have guessed at his age at thirty instead of the forty he claimed to be; now, studying his face closely, I could see that he had not exaggerated his age. One would have to laugh a long time to etch lines like those.

But he wasn't laughing now. He looked deadly serious, and he didn't look crazy. But he said something that sounded crazy.

He said, "Doctor, has it ever occurred to you that—that the fantasies of Lewis Carroll are not fantasies at all?"

"Do you mean," I asked, "in the sense that fantasy is often nearer to fundamental truth than is would-be realistic fiction?"

"No. I mean that they are literally, actually true. That they are not fiction at all, that they are reporting."

I stared at him. "If you think that, then who—or *what*—do you think Lewis Carroll was?"

27

He smiled faintly, but it wasn't a smile of amusement.

He said, "If you really want to know, and aren't afraid, you can find out tonight. There is a meeting, near here. Will you come?"

"May I be frank?"

"Certainly."

I said, "I think it's crazy, but try to keep me away."

"In spite of the fact that there is danger?"

Sure, I was going, danger or no. But maybe I could use his insistence on warning me to pry something out of him. So I said, "May I ask what *kind* of danger?"

He seemed to hesitate a moment and then he took out his wallet and from an inner compartment took a newspaper clipping, a short one of about three paragraphs. He handed it to me.

I read it, and I recognized the type and the setup; it was a clipping from the *Bridgeport Argus*. And I remembered how having read it, a couple of weeks ago, I'd considered clipping it as an exchange item, and then had decided not to, despite the fact that the heading had caught my interest. It read:

MAN SLAIN BY UNKNOWN BEAST

The facts were few and simple. A man named Colin Hawks, living outside Bridgeport, a recluse, had been found dead along a path through the woods. The man's throat had been torn, and police opinion was that a large and vicious dog had attacked him. But the reporter who wrote the article suggested the possibility that a wolf—or even a panther or a leopard—escaped from a circus or zoo might have caused the wounds.

I folded the clipping again and handed it back to Smith. It didn't mean anything, of course. It's easy to find stories like that if one looks for them. A man named Charles Fort found thousands of them and put them into four books he had written, books that were on my shelves.

This particular one was less mysterious than most. In fact, there wasn't any real mystery at all; undoubtedly some vicious dog had done the killing.

Just the same something prickled at the back of my neck.

It was the headline, really, not the article. It's funny what the word "unknown" and the thought back of it can do to you. If that story had

28

been headed "Man Killed by Vicious Dog"—or by a lion or a crocodile or any other specified creature, however fierce and dangerous, there'd have been nothing frightening about it.

But an *"unknown beast"*—well if you've got the same kind of imagination I have, you see what I mean. And if you haven't, I can't explain.

I looked at Yehudi Smith just in time to see him toss down his whisky—again like a conjuring trick. I handed him back the clipping and then refilled our glasses.

I said, "Interesting story. But where's the connection?"

"Our last meeting was in Bridgeport. That's all I can tell you. About that, I mean. You asked the nature of the danger; that's why I showed you that. And it's not too late for you to say no. It won't be, for that matter, until we get there."

"Get where?"

"Only a few miles from here. I have directions to guide me to a house on a road called the Dartown Pike. I have a car."

I said, irrelevantly, "So have I, but the tyres are flat. Two of them."

I thought about the Dartown Pike. I said. "You wouldn't, by any chance, be heading for the house known as the Wentworth place?"

"That's the name, yes. You know of it?"

Right then and there, if I'd been completely sober, I'd have seen that the whole thing was too good to be true. I'd have smelled a fish. Or blood.

I said, "We'll have to take candles or flashlights. That house has been empty since I was a kid. We used to call it a haunted house. Would that be why you chose it?"

"Yes, of course."

"And your group is meeting there tonight?"

He nodded. "At one o'clock in the morning, to be exact. You're sure you're not afraid?"

God, yes, I was afraid. Who wouldn't be, after the build-up he'd just handed me?

So I grinned at him and said, "Sure, I'm afraid. But just try to keep me away."

Then I had an idea. If I was going to a haunted house at one o'clock in the morning to hunt jabberwocks or try to invoke the ghost of Lewis

29

Carroll or some equally sensible thing, it wouldn't hurt to have someone along whom I already knew. And if Al Grainger dropped in—I tried to figure out whether or not Al would be interested. He was a Carroll fan, all right, but—for the rest of it, I didn't know.

I said, "One question, Mr. Smith. A young friend of mine might drop in soon for a game of chess. How exclusive is this deal? I mean, would it be all right if he came along, if he wants to?"

"Do you think he's qualified?"

"Depends on what the qualifications are," I said. "Offhand, I'd say you have to be a Lewis Carroll fan and a little crazy. Or, come to think of it, are those one and the same qualification?"

He laughed. "They're not too far apart. But tell me something about your friend. You said young friend; how young?"

"About twenty-three. Not long out of college. Good literary taste and background, which means he knows and likes Carroll. He can quote almost as much of it as I can. Plays chess, if that's a qualification—and I'd guess it is. Dodgson not only played chess but based *Through the Looking-Glass* on a chess game. His name, if that matters, is Al Grainger."

"Would he *want* to come?"

"Frankly," I admitted, "I haven't an idea on that angle."

Smith said, "I hope he comes; if he's a Carroll enthusiast, I'd like to meet him. But, if he comes, will you do me a favour of saying nothing about—what I've told you, at least until I've had a chance to judge him a bit? Frankly, it would be almost unprecedented if I took the liberty of inviting someone to an important meeting like tonight's on my own. You're being invited because we know quite a bit about you. You were voted on—and I might say that the vote to invite you was unanimous."

I remembered his familiarity with the two obscure things about Lewis Carroll that I'd written, and I didn't doubt that he—or they, if he really represented a group—did know something about me.

He said, "But—well, if I get a chance to meet him and think he'd really fit in, I might take a chance and ask him. Can you tell me anything more about him? What does he do—for a living I mean?"

That was harder to answer. I said, "Well, he's writing plays. But I don't think he makes a living at it; in fact, I don't know that he's ever sold any. He's a bit of a mystery to Carmel City. He's lived here all his life—except while he was away at college—and nobody knows where his money comes from. Has a swanky car and a place of his own—he lived there with his mother until she died a few years ago—and seems to have plenty of spending money, but nobody knows where it comes from." I grinned. "And it annoys the hell out of Carmel City not to know. You know how small towns are."

He nodded. "Wouldn't it be a logical assumption that he inherited the money?"

"From one point of view, yes. But it doesn't seem too likely. His mother worked all her life as a milliner, and without owning her own shop. The town, I remember, used to wonder how she managed to own her own house and send her son to college on what she earned. But she couldn't possibly have earned enough to have done both of those things and still have left him enough money to have supported him in idleness—Well, maybe writing plays isn't idleness, but it isn't remunerative unless you sell them—for several years."

I shrugged. "But there's probably no mystery to it. She must have had an income from investments her husband had made, and Al either inherited the income or got the capital from which it came. He probably doesn't talk about his business because he enjoys being mysterious."

"Was his father wealthy?"

"His father died before he was born, and before Mrs. Grainger moved to Carmel City. So nobody here knew his father. And I guess that's all I can tell you about Al, except that he can beat me at chess most of the time, and that I hope you'll have a chance to meet him."

Smith nodded. "If he comes, we'll see."

He glanced at his empty glass and I took the hint and filled it and my own. Again I watched the incredible manner of his drinking it, fascinated. I'd swear that, this time, the glass came no closer than six inches from his lips. Definitely it was a trick I'd have to learn myself. If for no other reason than that I don't really like the taste of whisky, much as I enjoy the effects of it. With his way of drinking, it didn't seem that he had the slightest chance of tasting the stuff. It was there, in the glass, and then it was gone. His Adam's apple didn't seem to work and if he was talking at the time he drank there was scarcely an interruption in what he was saying.

The phone rang. I excused myself and answered it.

"Doc," said Clyde Andrews' voice, "this is Clyde Andrews."

"Fine," I said, "I suppose you realize that you sabotaged this week's issue by cancelling a story on my front page. What's called off this time?"

"I'm sorry about that, Doc, if it really inconvenienced you, but with the sale called off, I thought you wouldn't want to run the story and have people coming around to——"

"Of course," I interrupted him. I was impatient to get back to my conversation with Yehudi Smith. "That's all right, Clyde. But what do you want now?"

"I want to know if you've decided whether or not you want to sell the *Clarion.*"

For a second I was unreasonably angry. I said, "God damn it, Clyde, you interrupt the only real conversation I've had in years to ask me that, when we've been talking about it for months, off and on? I don't know. I do and I don't want to sell it."

"Sorry for heckling you, Doc, but I just got a special delivery letter from my brother in Ohio. He's got an offer out West. Says he'd rather come to Carmel City on the proposition I'd made to him—contingent on your deciding to sell me the *Clarion,* of course. But he's got to accept the other offer right away—within a day or so, that is—if he's going to accept it at all.

"So you see that makes it different, Doc. I've got to know right away. Not tonight, necessarily; it isn't in that much of a rush. But I've got to know by tomorrow sometime, so I thought I'd call you right away so you could start coming to a decision."

I nodded and then realized that he couldn't see me nod so I said, "Sure, Clyde, I get it. I'm sorry for popping off. All right, I'll make up my mind by tomorrow morning. I'll let you know one way or the other by then. Okay?"

"Fine," he said. "That'll be plenty of time. Oh, by the way, there's an item of news for you if it's not too late to put it in. Or have you already got it?"

"Got what?"

"About the escaped maniac. I don't know the details, but a friend of mine just drove over from Neilsville and he says they're stopping cars and

32

watching the roads both sides of the country asylum. Guess you can get the details if you call the asylum."

"Thanks, Clyde," I said.

I put the phone back down in its cradle and looked at Yehudi Smith. I wondered why, with all the fantastic things he'd said, I hadn't already guessed.

CHAPTER FOUR

"But wait a bit," the Oyster cried,
"Before we have our chat;
For some of us are out of breath,
And all of us are fat!"

I FELT a hell of a letdown. Oh, not that I'd really quite believed in the Vorpal Blades or that we were going to a haunted house to conjure up a Jabberwock or whatever we'd have done there.

But it had been exciting even to think about it, just as one can get excited over a chess game even though he knows that the kings and queens on the board aren't real entities and that when a bishop slays a knight no real blood is shed. I guess it had been that kind of excitement, the vicarious kind, that I'd felt about the things Yehudi Smith had promised. Or maybe a better comparison would be that it had been like reading an exciting fiction story that one knows isn't true but which one can believe in for as long as the story lasts.

Now there wasn't even that. Across from me, I realized with keen disappointment, was only a man who'd escaped from an insane asylum. Yehudi, the little man who wasn't there—mentally.

The funny part of it was that I still liked him. He was a nice little guy and he'd given me a fascinating half hour, up to now. I hated the fact that I'd have to turn him over to the asylum guards and have him put back where he came from.

Well, I thought, at least it would give me a news story to fill that nine-inch hole in the front page of the *Clarion*.

He said, "I hope the call wasn't anything that will spoil our plans, Doctor."

It had spoiled more than that, but of course I couldn't tell him so, any more than I could have told Clyde Andrews over the phone, in Smith's presence to call the asylum and tell them to drop around to my house if they wanted to collect their bolted nut.

So I shook my head while I figured out an angle to get out of the house and to put in the phone call from next door.

I stood up. Perhaps I was a bit more drunk than I'd thought, for I had to catch my balance. I remember how crystal clear my mind seemed to be—but of course nothing seems more crystal clear than a prism that makes you see around corners.

I said, "No, the call won't interrupt our plans except for a few minutes. I've got to give a message to the man next door. Excuse me—and help yourself to the whisky."

I went through the kitchen and outside into the black night. There were lights in the houses on either side of me, and I wondered which of my neighbours to bother. And then I wondered why I was in such a hurry to bother either of them.

Surely, I thought, the man who called himself Yehudi Smith wasn't dangerous. And, crazy or not, he was the most interesting man I'd met in years. He *did* seem to know something about Lewis Carroll. And I remembered again that he'd known about my obscure brochure and equally obscure magazine article. How?

So, come to think of it, why shouldn't I stall making that phone call for another hour or so, and relax and enjoy myself? Now that I was over the first disappointment of learning that he was insane, why wouldn't I find talk about the delusion of his almost as interesting as though it was factual?

Interesting in a different way, of course. Often I had thought I'd like the chance to talk to a paranoiac about his delusions—neither arguing with him nor agreeing with him, just trying to find out what made him tick.

And the evening was still a pup; it couldn't be later than about half past eight so my neighbours would be up at least another hour or two.

So why was I in a hurry to make that call? I wasn't.

Of course I had to kill enough time outside to make it reasonable to believe that I'd actually gone next door and delivered a message, so I stood there at the bottom of my back steps, looking up at the black velvet sky, star-studded but moonless, and wondering what was behind it and why madmen were mad. And how strange it would be if one of them was right and all the rest of us were crazy instead.

Then I went back inside and I was cowardly enough to do a ridiculous thing. From the kitchen I went into my bedroom and to my closet. In a shoebox on the top shelf was a short-barrelled thirty-eight calibre revolver, one of the compact, lightweight models they call a Banker's Special. I'd never shot at anything with it and hoped that I never would—and I wasn't sure I could hit anything smaller than an elephant or farther away than a couple of yards. I don't even like guns. I hadn't bought this one; an acquaintance had once borrowed twenty bucks from me and had insisted on my taking the pistol for security. And later he'd wanted another five and said if I gave it to him I could keep the gun. I hadn't wanted it, but he'd needed the five pretty badly and I'd given it to him.

It was still loaded with bullets that were in it when we'd made the deal four or five years ago, and I didn't know whether they'd still shoot or not, but I put it in my trouser pocket. I wouldn't use it, of course, except in dire extremity—and I'd miss anything I shot at even then, but I thought that just carrying the gun would make my coming conversation seem dangerous and exciting, more than it would be otherwise.

I went into the living-room and he was still there. He hadn't poured himself a drink, so I poured one for each of us and then sat down on the sofa again.

I lifted my drink and over the rim of it watched him do that marvellous trick again—just a toss of the glass toward his lips. I drank my own less spectacularly and said, "I wish I had a movie camera. I'd like to film the way you do that and then study it in slow motion."

He laughed. "Afraid it's my one way of showing off. I used to be a juggler once."

"And now? If you don't mind my asking."

"A student," he said. "A student of Lewis Carroll—and mathematics."

"Is there a living in it?" I asked him.

He hesitated just a second. "Do you mind if I defer answering that until you've learned—what you'll learn at tonight's meeting?"

Of course there wasn't going to be any meeting tonight; I knew that now. But I said, "Not at all. But I hope you don't mean that we can't talk about Carroll, in general, until after the meeting."

I hoped he'd give the right answer to that; it would mean that I could get him going on the subject of his mania.

He said, "Of course not. In fact, I *want* to talk about him. There are facts I want to give you that will enable you to understand things better. Some of the facts you already know, but I'll refresh you on them anyway. For instance, dates. You had his birth and death dates correct, or nearly enough so. But do you know the dates of the Alice books or any other of his works? The sequence is important."

"Not exactly," I told him. "I think that he wrote the first Alice book when he was comparatively young, about thirty."

"Close. He was thirty-two. *Alice in Wonderland* was published in eighteen sixty-three, but even before then he was on the trail of something. Do you know what he had published before that?"

I shook my head.

"Two books. He wrote and published *A Syllabus of Plane Geometry* in eighteen sixty and in the year after that his *Formulae of Plane Trigonometry*. Have you read either of them?"

I had to shake my head again. I said, "Mathematics isn't my forte. I've read only his non-technical books."

He smiled. "There aren't any. You simply failed to recognize the mathematics embodied in the Alice books and in his poetry. You do know, I'm sure, that many of his poems are acrostics."

"Of course."

"All of them are acrostics, but in a much more subtle manner. However, I can see why you failed to find the clues if you haven't read his treatises on mathematics. You wouldn't have read his *Elementary Treatise on Determinants,* I suppose. But how about his *Curiosa Mathematical"*

I hated to disappoint him again, but I had to.

He frowned at me. "That at least you should have read. It's not technical at all, and most of the clues to the fantasies are contained in it. There are further—and final—references to them in his *Symbolic Logic,* published in eighteen ninety-six, just two years before his death, but they are less direct."

I said, "Now, wait a minute. If I understand you correctly your thesis is that Lewis Carroll—leaving aside any question of who or what he really was—worked out through mathematics and expressed in fantasy the fact that—what?"

"That there is another plane of existence besides the one we are now living in. That we can have—and do sometimes have—access to it."

"But what kind of a plane? A through-the-looking-glass plane of fantasy, a dream plane?"

"Exactly, Doctor. A dream plane. That isn't strictly accurate, but it's about as nearly as I can explain it to you just yet." He leaned forward. "Consider dreams. Aren't they the almost perfect parallel of the Alice adventures? The wool-and-water sequence, for instance, where everything Alice looks at changes into something else. Remember in the shop, with the old sheep knitting, how Alice looked hard to see what was on the shelves, but the shelf she looked at was always empty although the others about it were always full—of something, and she never found out what?"

I nodded slowly. I said, "Her comment was, 'Things flow about so here.' And then the sheep asked if Alice could row and handed her a pair of knitting needles and the needles turned into oars in her hands and she was in a boat, with the sheep still knitting."

"Exactly, Doctor. A perfect dream sequence. And consider that *Jabberwocky*—which is probably the best thing in the second Alice book—is in the very *language* of dreams. It's full of words like *frumious, manxome, tulgey,* words that give you a perfect picture in context—but you can't put your finger on what the context is. In a dream you fully understand such meanings, but you forget them when you awaken."

Between *"manxome"* and *"tulgey",* he'd downed his latest drink. I didn't pour another this time; I was beginning to wonder how long the bottle—or we—would last. But he showed no effect whatsoever from the drinks he'd been downing. I can't quite say the same for myself. I knew my voice was getting a bit thick.

I said, "But why postulate the *reality* of such a world? I can see your point otherwise. The Jabberwock itself is the epitome of nightmare creatures—with eyes of flame and jaws that bite and claws that catch, and it whiffles and burbles—why, Freud and James Joyce in tandem couldn't have done any better. But why not take it that Lewis Carroll was trying, and damned successfully, to write as in a dream? Why make the assumption that that world is real? Why talk of getting through to it—except, of course, in the sense that we invade it nightly in our dreams?"

He smiled. "Because that world *is* real, Doctor. You'll hear evidence of that tonight, mathematical evidence. And, I hope, actual proof. I've had such proof myself, and I hope you'll have. But you'll see the calculations, at least, and it will be explained to you how they were derived from *Curiosa Mathematica,* and then corroborated by evidence found in the other books.

"Carroll was more than a century ahead of his time. Doctor. Have you read of the recent experiments with the subconscious made by Leibnitz and Winton—the feelers they're putting forth in the right direction, which is the mathematical approach?"

I admitted I hadn't heard of Liebnitz or Winton.

"They aren't well known," he conceded. "You see, only recently, except for Carroll, has anyone even considered the possibility of our reaching—let's call it the dream plane until I've shown you what it really is—physically as well as mentally."

"As Lewis Carroll reached it?"

"As he must have, to have known the things he knew. Things so revolutionary and dangerous that he did not dare reveal them openly."

For a fleeting moment it sounded so reasonable that I wondered if it *could* be true. Why not? Why couldn't there be other dimensions beside our own? Why couldn't a brilliant mathematician with a fantastic mind have found a way through to one of them?

In my mind, I cussed out Clyde Andrews for having told me about the asylum break. If only I hadn't learned about that, what a wonderful evening this one would be. Even knowing Smith was insane, I found myself—possibly with the whisky's help—wondering if he could be right. How marvellous it would have been without the knowledge of his insanity to temper the wonder and the wondering. It would have been an evening in Wonderland.

And, sane or crazy, I liked him. Sane or crazy, he belonged figuratively in the department in which Mrs. Carr's husband worked literally. I laughed and then, of course, I had to explain what I'd been laughing about.

His eyes lighted. "The Roman candle department. That's marvellous. The Roman candle department."

You see what I mean.

We had a drink to the Roman candle department, and then it happened that neither of us said anything right away and it was so quiet that I jumped when the phone rang.

I picked it up and said into it, "This is the Roman candle department."

"Doc?" It was the voice of Pete Corey, my printer. It sounded tense. "I've got bad news."

Pete doesn't get excited easily. I sobered up a little and asked, "What, Pete?"

"Listen, Doc. Remember just a couple of hours ago you were saying you wished a murder or something would happen so you'd have a story for the paper—and remember how I asked you if you'd like one even if it happened to a friend of yours?"

Of course I remembered; he'd mentioned my best friend, Carl Trenholm. I took a tighter grip on the phone. I said, "Cut out breaking it gently, Pete. Has something happened to Carl?"

"Yes, Doc."

"For God's sake, what? Cut the build-up. Is he dead?"

"That's what I heard. He was found out on the pike; I don't know if he was hit by a car or what."

"Where is he now?"

"Being brought in, I guess. All I know is that Hank called me"—Hank is Pete's brother-in-law and a deputy sheriff—"and said they got a call from someone who found him alongside the road out there. Even Hank had it third-hand—Rance Kates phoned him and said to come down and take care of the office while he went out there. And Hank knows Kates doesn't like you and wouldn't give you the tip, so Hank called me. But don't get Hank in trouble with his boss by telling anybody where the tip came from."

"Did you call the hospital?" I asked. "If Carl's just hurt——"

"Wouldn't be time for them to get him there yet—or to wherever they do take him. Hank just phoned me from his own place before he started for the sheriff's office, and Kates had just called him from the office and was just leaving there."

"Okay, Peter," I said. "Thanks. I'm going back downtown; I'll call the hospital from the *Clarion* office. You call me there if you hear anything more."

"Hell, Doc, I'm coming down too."

I told him he didn't have to, but he said the hell with having to; he wanted to. I didn't argue with him.

I cradled the phone and found that I was already standing up. I said, "Sorry, but something important's come up—an accident to a friend of mine." I headed for the closet to get my coat. "Do you want to wait here, or——"

"If you don't mind," he said. "That is, if you think you won't be very long."

"I don't know that, but I'll phone here and let you know as soon as I can. If the phone rings answer it; it'll be me. And help yourself to whisky and books."

He nodded. "I'll get along fine. Hope your friend isn't seriously hurt."

That was all that I was worrying about myself. I put on my hat and hurried out, again, and this time seriously, cussing those two flat tyres on my car and the fact that I hadn't taken time to fix them that morning. Nine blocks isn't far to walk when you're not in a hurry, but it's a hell of a distance when you're anxious to get there quickly.

I walked fast, so fast, in fact, that I winded myself in the first two blocks and had to slow down.

I kept thinking the same thing Pete had obviously thought—what a hell of a coincidence it was that we'd mentioned the possibility of Carl's being——

But we'd been talking about murder. Had Carl been murdered? Of course not; things like that didn't happen in Carmel City. It must have been an accident, a hit-run driver. No one would have the slightest reason for killing, of all people, Carl Trenholm. No one but a——

Finishing that thought made me stop walking suddenly. *No one but a maniac* would have the slightest reason for killing Carl Trenholm. But there was an escaped maniac at large tonight and—unless he'd left instead of waiting for me—he was sitting right in my living-room. I'd thought he was harmless—even though I'd taken the precaution of putting that gun in my pocket—but how could I be sure? I'm no psychiatrist; where did I get the bright idea that I could tell the difference between a harmless nut and a homicidal maniac?

I started to turn back and then realized that going back was useless and foolish. He would either have left as soon as I was out of sight around the corner, or he hadn't guessed that I suspected him and would wait as I'd told him to, until he heard from me. So all I had to do was to phone the asylum as soon as I could and they'd send guards to close in on my house and take him if he was still there.

I started walking again. Yes, it would be ridiculous for me to go back alone, even though I still had that gun in my pocket. He might resist, and I wouldn't want to have to use the gun, especially as I hadn't any real reason to believe he'd killed Carl. It could have been an auto accident just as easily; I couldn't even form an intelligent opinion on that until I learned what Carl's injuries were.

I kept walking, as fast as I could without winding myself again.

Suddenly I thought of that newspaper clipping—"MAN SLAIN BY UNKNOWN BEAST." A prickle went down my spine—*what if Carl's body showed*——

And then the horrible thought pyramided. What if the *unknown beast* who had killed the man near Bridgeport and the escaped maniac were one and the same. What if he had escaped before at the time of the killing at Bridgeport—or, for that matter, hadn't been committed to the asylum until after that killing, whether or not he was suspected of it.

I thought of lycanthropy, and shivered. *What* might I have been talking about Jabberwocks and unknown beasts with?

Suddenly the gun I'd put in my pocket felt comforting there. I looked around over my shoulder to be sure that nothing was coming after me. The street behind was empty, but I started walking a little faster just the same.

Suddenly the street lights weren't bright enough and the night, which had been a pleasant June evening, was a frightful, menacing thing. I was really scared. Maybe it's as well that I didn't guess that things hadn't even started to happen.

I felt glad that I was passing the courthouse—with a light on in the window of the sheriffs office. I even considered going in. Probably Hank would be there by now and Rance Kates would still be gone. But no, I was this far now and I'd carry on to the *Clarion* office and start my phoning from there. Besides, if Kates found out I'd been in his office talking to Hank, Hank would be in trouble.

So I kept on going. The corner of Oak Street, and I turned, now only a block and a half from the *Clarion*. But it was going to take me quite a while to make that block and a half.

A big, dark blue Buick sedan suddenly pulled near the kerb and slowed down alongside me. There were two men in the front seat and the one who was driving stuck his head out of the window and said, "Hey, Buster, what town is this?"

CHAPTER FIVE

When the sands are all dry, he is gay as a lark
And will talk in contemptuous tones of the Shark;
But, when the tide rises and sharks are around,
His voice has a timid and tremulous sound.

It had been a long time since anyone had called me "Buster," and I didn't particularly like it. I didn't like the looks of the men, either, or the tone of voice the question had been asked in. A minute ago, I'd thought I'd be glad of any company short of that of the escaped maniac; now I decided differently.

I'm not often rude, but I can be when someone else starts it. I said, "Sorry, pal, I'm a stranger here myself." And I kept on walking.

I heard the man behind the wheel of the Buick say something to the other, and then they passed me and swung in to the kerb just ahead. The driver got out and walked toward me.

I stopped short and tried not to do a double-take when I recognized him. My attention to the wanted circulars on the post office bulletin board was about to pay off—although from the expression on his face, the pay off wasn't going to be the kind I'd want.

The man coming toward me and only two steps away when I stopped was Bat Masters, whose picture had been posted only last week and was still there on the board. I couldn't be wrong about his face, and I remembered the name clearly because of its similarity to the name of Bat Masterson, the famous gunman of the old West. I'd thought of it as a coincidence at first and then I realized that the similarity of Masters to Masterton had made the nickname "Bat" a natural.

He was a big man with a long, horselike face, eyes wide apart and a mouth that was a narrow straight line separating a lantern jaw from a wide upper lip; on the latter there was a two-day stubble of hair that indicated he was starting a moustache. But it would have taken plastic surgery and a full beard to disguise that face from anyone who had recently, however casually, studied a picture of it. Bat Masters, bank robber and killer.

I had the gun in my pocket, but I didn't remember it at the time. It's probably just as well; if I'd remembered, I might have been frightened into reaching for it. And that probably would not have been a healthful thing to do. He was coming at me with his fists balled but no gun in either of them. He didn't intend to kill me—although one of those fists might do it quite easily and unintentionally: I weigh a hundred and forty wringing wet, and he weighed almost twice that and had shoulders that bulged out his suit coat.

There wasn't even time to turn and run. His left hand came out and caught the front of my coat and pulled me toward him, almost lifting me off the sidewalk.

He said, "Listen, Pop, I don't want any lip. I asked you a question."

"Carmel City," I said. "Carmel City, Illinois."

The voice of the other man, still in the car, came back to us.

"Hey, Bill, don't hurt the guy. We don't want to———" He didn't finish the sentence, of course; to say you don't want to attract attention is the best way of drawing it.

Masters looked past me—right over my head—to see if anybody or anything was coming that way and then, still keeping his grip on the front of my coat, turned and looked the other way. He wasn't afraid of my swinging at him enough to bother keeping his eyes on me, and I didn't blame him for feeling that way about it.

A car was coming now, about a block away. And two men came out of the drugstore on the opposite side of the street, only a few buildings down. Then behind me I could hear the sound of another car turning into Oak Street.

Masters turned back to me and let go, so we were just two men standing there face to face if anyone noticed us. He said, "Okay, Pop. Next time somebody asks you a question, don't be so God damn fresh."

He still glared at me as though he hadn't yet completely given up the idea of giving me something to remember him by—maybe just a light open-handed slap that wouldn't do anything worse than crack my jaw-bone and drive my dentures down my throat.

I said, "Sure, sorry," and let my voice sound afraid, but tried not to sound quite as afraid as I really was—because if he even remotely suspected that I might have recognized him, I wasn't going to get out of it at all.

He swung around and walked back to the car, got in and drove off. I suppose I should have got the licence number, but it would have been a stolen car anyway—and besides I didn't think of it. I didn't even watch the car as it drove away; if either of them looked back I didn't want them to think I was giving them what criminals call the big-eye. I didn't want to give them any possible reason to change their minds about going on.

I started walking again, keeping to the middle of the sidewalk and trying to look like a man minding his own business. Also trying to keep my knees from shaking so hard that I couldn't walk at all.

It had been a narrow squeak all right. If the street had been completely empty——

I could have notified the sheriffs office about a minute quicker by turning around and going back that way, but I didn't take the chance. If someone was watching me out of the back window of the car, a change in direction wouldn't be a good idea. There was a difference of only a block anyway; I was half a block past the courthouse and a block and a half away from Smiley's and the *Clarion* office across the street from it. From either one I could phone in the big news that Bat Masters and a companion had just driven through Carmel City heading north, probably toward Chicago. And Hank Ganzer, in the sheriffs office, would relay the story to the state police and there was probably better than an even chance that they'd be caught within an hour or two.

And if they were, I might even get a slice of the reward for giving the tip—but I didn't care as much about that as about the story I was going to have. Why, it was a story, even if they weren't caught, and if they were, it would be a really big one. And a local story—if the tip came from Carmel City—even if they were actually caught several counties north. Maybe there'd even be a gun battle—from my all too close look at Masters I had a hunch that there would be.

46

Perfect timing, too, I thought. For once something was happening on a Thursday night. For once I'd beat the Chicago papers. They'd have the story, too, of course, and a lot of Carmel City people take Chicago dailies, but they don't come in until the late afternoon train and the *Clarion* would be out hours before that.

Yes, for once I was going to have a newspaper with *news* in it. Even if Masters and his pal weren't caught, the fact that they'd passed through town made a story. And besides that, there was the escaped maniac, and Carl Trenholm——

Thinking about Carl again made me walk faster. It was safe by now; I'd gone a quarter of a block since the Buick had driven off. It wasn't anywhere in sight and again the street was quiet; thank God it hadn't been this quiet while Masters had been making up his mind whether or not to slug me.

I was past Deak's Music Store, dark. Past the super-market, ditto. The bank——

I had passed the bank, too, when I stopped as suddenly as though I'd run into a wall. The bank had been dark too. And it shouldn't have been; there's a small night light that always burns over the safe. I'd passed the bank thousands of times after dark and never before had the light been off.

For a moment the wild thought went through my head that Bat and his companion must have just burglarized the bank—although robbery, not burglary, was Masters' trade—and then I saw how ridiculous that thought had been. They'd been driving toward the bank and a quarter of a block away from it when they'd stopped to ask me what town they were in. True, they could have burglarized the bank and then circled the block in their car, but if they had they'd have been intent on their getaway. Criminals do pretty silly things, sometimes, but not quite so silly as to stop a getaway car within spitting distance of the scene of the crime to ask what town they're in, and then to top it by getting out of the car to slug a random pedestrian because they don't like his answers to their question.

No, Masters and company couldn't have robbed the bank. And they wouldn't be burglarizing it now, either. Their car had gone on past; I hadn't watched it, but my ears had told me that it had kept on going. And even if it hadn't, I had. My encounter with them had been only seconds ago; there wasn't possibly time for them to have broken in there, even if they'd stopped.

I went back a few steps and looked into the window of the bank.

At first I saw nothing except the vague silhouette of a window at the back—the top half of the window, that is, which was visible above the counter. Then the silhouette became less vague and I could see that the window had been opened; the top bar of the lower sash showed clearly, only a few inches from the top of the frame.

That was the means of entry all right—but was the burglar still in there, or had he left, and left the window open behind him?

I strained my eyes against the blackness to the left of the window, where the safe was. And suddenly a dim light flickered briefly, as though a match had been struck but had gone out before the phosphorus had ignited the wood. I could see only the brief light of it, as it was below the level of the counter; I couldn't see whoever had lighted it.

The burglar was still there.

And suddenly I was running on tiptoe back through the areaway between the bank and post office.

Good God, don't ask me *why*. Sure, I had money in the bank, but the bank had insurance against burglary and it wasn't any skin off my backside if the bank was robbed. I wasn't even thinking that it would be a better story for the *Clarion* if I got the burglar—or if he got me. I just wasn't thinking at all. I was running back alongside the bank toward that window that he'd left open for his getaway.

I think it must have been reaction from the cowardice I'd shown and felt only a minute before. I must have been a bit punch drunk from Jabberwocks and Vorpal Blades and homicidal maniacs with lycanthropy and bank bandits and a bank burglar—or maybe I thought I'd suddenly been promoted to the Roman candle department.

Maybe I was drunk, maybe I was a little mentally unbalanced—use any maybe you want, but there I was running tiptoe through the areaway. Running, that is, as far as the light from the street would let me; then I groped along the side of the building until I came to the alley. There was dim light there, enough for me to be able to see the window.

It was still open.

48

I stood there looking at it and vaguely beginning to realize how crazy I'd been. Why hadn't I run to the sheriff's office for Hank? The burglar—or, for all I knew, burglars—might be just starting his work on the safe in there. He might be in a long time, long enough for Hank to get here and collar him. If he came out now, what was I going to do about it? Shoot him? That was ridiculous; I'd rather let him get away with robbing the bank than do that.

And then it was too late because suddenly there was a soft shuffling sound from the window and a hand appeared on the sill. He was coming out, and there wasn't a chance that I could get away without his hearing me. What would happen then, I didn't know. I would just as soon not find out.

A moment before, just as I'd reached the place beside the window where I now stood, I'd stepped on a piece of wood, a one-by-two stick of it about a foot long. That was a weapon I could understand. I reached down and grabbed it and swung, just in time, as a head came through the window.

Thank God I didn't swing too hard. At the last second, even in that faint light, I'd thought—

The head and the hand weren't in the window any more and there was the soft thud of a body falling inside. There wasn't any sound or movement for seconds. Long seconds, and then there was the sound of my stick of wood hitting the dirt of the alley and I knew I'd dropped it.

If it hadn't been for what I'd thought I'd seen in the last fraction of a second before it was too late to stop the blow, I could have run now for the sheriff's office. But——

Maybe here went *my* head, but I had to chance it. The sill of the window wasn't much over waist high. I leaned across it and struck a match, and I'd been right.

I climbed in the window and felt for his heart and it was beating all right. He seemed to be breathing normally. I ran my hands very gently over his head and then held them in the open window to look at them; there wasn't any blood. There could be, then, nothing worse than a concussion.

I lowered the window so nobody would notice that it was open and then I felt my way carefully toward the nearest desk—I'd been in the bank thousands of times; I knew its layout—and groped for a telephone until I found one.

The operator's voice said, "Number please?" and I started to give it and then remembered; she'd know where the call came from and that the bank was closed. Naturally, she'd listen in. Maybe she'd even call the sheriff's office to tell them someone was using the telephone in the bank.

Had I recognised her voice? I'd thought I had. I said, "Is that Milly?"

"Yes. Is this—Mr. Stoeger?"

"Right," I said. I was glad she'd known *my* voice. "Listen, Milly, I'm calling from the bank, but it's all right. You don't need to worry about it. And—do me a favour, will you? Please don't listen in."

"All right, Mr. Stoeger. Sure. What number do you want?"

I gave it; the number of Clyde Andrews, president of the bank. As I heard the ringing of the phone at the other end, I thought how lucky it was that I'd known Milly all her life and that we liked one another. I knew that she'd be burning with curiosity but that she wouldn't listen in.

Clyde Andrew's voice answered. I was still careful about what I said because I didn't know offhand whether he was on a party line.

I said, "This is Doc Stoeger, Clyde. I'm down at the bank. Get down here right away. Hurry."

"Huh? Doc, are you drunk or something? What would you be doing at the bank. It's closed."

I said, "Somebody was inside here. I hit him over the head with a piece of wood when he started back out of the window, and he's unconscious but not hurt bad. But just to be sure, pick up Doc Minton on your way here. And hurry."

"Sure," he said, "Are you phoning the sheriff or shall I?"

"Neither of us. Don't phone anybody. Just get Minton and get here quick."

"But——I don't get it. Why not phone the sheriff? Is this a gag?"

I said, "No, Clyde. Listen—you'll want to see the burglar first. He isn't badly hurt, but for God's sake quit arguing and get down here with Dr. Minton. Do you understand?"

His tone of voice was different when he said, "I'll be there. Five minutes."

I put the receiver back on the phone and then lifted it again. The "Number, please" was Milly's voice again and I asked her if she knew anything about Carl Trenholm.

She didn't; she hadn't known anything had happened at all. When I told her what little I knew she said yes, that she'd routed a call from a farmhouse out on the pike to the sheriffs office about half an hour before, but she'd had several other calls around the same time and hadn't listened in on it.

I decided that I'd better wait until I was somewhere else before I called to report either Bat Masters' passing through or about the escaped maniac at my own house. It wouldn't be safe to risk making the call from here, and a few more minutes wouldn't matter a lot.

I went back, groping my way through the dark toward the dim square of the window, and bent down again by the boy, Clyde Andrews' son. His breathing and his heart were still okay and he moved a little and muttered something as though he was coming out of it. I don't know anything about concussion, but I thought that was a good sign and felt better. It would have been terrible if I'd swung a little harder and had killed him or injured him seriously.

I sat down on the floor so my head would be out of the line of sight if anyone looked in the front window, as I had a few minutes before, and waited.

So much had been happening that I felt a little numb. There was so much to think about that I guess I didn't think about any of it. I just sat there in the dark.

When the phone rang I jumped about two feet.

I groped to it and answered. Milly's voice said, "Mr. Stoeger, I thought I'd better tell you if you're still there. Somebody from the drugstore across the street just phoned the sheriff's office and said the night light in the bank is out, and whoever answered at the sheriffs office—it sounded like one of the deputies, not Mr. Kates—said they'd come right around."

I said, "Thanks, Milly. Thanks a lot."

A car was pulling up at the kerb outside; I could see it through the window. I breathed a sigh of relief when I recognized the men getting out of it as Clyde Andrews and the doctor.

I switched on the lights inside while Clyde was unlocking the front door. I told him quickly about the call that had been made to the sheriff's office while I was leading them back to where Harvey Andrews was lying. We moved him slightly to a point where neither he nor Dr. Minton, bending over him, could be seen from the front of the bank, and we did it just in time. Hank was rapping on the door.

I stayed out of sight, too, to avoid having to explain what I was doing there. I heard Clyde Andrews open the door for Hank and explain that everything was all right, that someone had phoned him, too, that the night light was out and that he'd just got here to check up and that the bulb had merely burned out.

When Hank left, Clyde came back, his face a bit white. Dr. Minton said, "He's going to be all right, Clyde. Starting to come out of it. Soon as he can walk between us, we'll get him to the hospital for a checkup and be sure."

I said, "Clyde, I've got to run. There's a lot popping tonight. But as soon as you're sure the boy's all right will you let me know? I'll probably be at the *Clarion*, but I might be at Smiley's—or if it's a long time from now, I might be home."

"Sure, Doc." He put his hand on my shoulder. "And thanks a lot for—calling me instead of the sheriff's office."

"That's all right," I told him. "And, Clyde, I didn't know who it was before I hit. He was coming out of the back window and I thought——"

Clyde said, "I looked in his room after you phoned. He'd packed. I—I can't understand it, Doc. He's only fifteen. Why he'd do a thing like——" He shook his head. "He's always been headstrong and he's got into little troubles a few times, but—I don't understand this." He looked at me very earnestly. "Do you?"

I thought maybe I did understand a little of it, but I was remembering about Bat Masters and the fact that he was getting farther away every minute and that I'd better get the state police notified pretty quickly.

So I said, "Can I talk to you about it tomorrow, Clyde? Get the boy's side of it when he can talk—and just try to keep your mind open until then. I think—it may not be as bad as you think right now."

I left him still looking like a man who's just taken an almost mortal blow, and went out.

I headed down the street thinking what a damn fool I'd been to do what I'd done. But then, where had I missed a chance to do something wrong anywhere down the line tonight? And then, on second thought, this one thing might not have been wrong. If I'd called Hank, the boy just might have been shot instead of knocked out. And in any case he'd have been arrested.

That would have been bad. This way, there was a chance he could be straightened out before it was too late. Maybe a psychiatrist could help him. The only thing was, Clyde Andrews would have to realize that he, too, would have to take advice from the psychiatrist. He was a good man, but a hard father. You can't expect the things of a fifteen-year-old boy that Clyde expected of Harvey, and not have something go wrong somewhere down the line. But burglarizing a bank, even his own father's bank—I couldn't make up my mind whether that made it better or worse—was certainly something I hadn't looked for. It appalled me, a bit. Harvey's running away from home wouldn't have surprised me at all; I don't know that I'd even have blamed him.

A man can be too good a man and too conscientious and strict a father for his son ever to be able to love him. If Clyde Andrews would only get drunk—good and stinking drunk—just once in his life, he might get an entirely different perspective on things, even if he never again took another drink. But he'd never taken a drink yet, not one in his whole life. I don't think he'd ever smoked a cigarette or said a naughty word.

I liked him anyway; I'm pretty tolerant, I guess. But I'm glad I hadn't had a father like him. In my books, the man in town who was the best father was Carl Trenholm. Trenholm—and I hadn't found out yet whether he was dead or only injured!

I was only half a block, now, from Smiley's and the *Clarion*. I broke into a trot. Even at my age, it wouldn't wind me to trot that far. It had probably been less than half an hour since I'd left home, but with the things that had happened *en route,* it seemed like days. Well, anyway, nothing could happen to me between here and Smiley's. And nothing did.

I could see through the glass that there weren't any customers at the bar and that Smiley was alone behind it. Polishing glasses, as always; I think he must polish the same glasses a dozen times over when there's nothing else for him to do.

I burst in and headed for the telephone. I said, "Smiley, hell's popping tonight. There's an escaped lunatic, and something's happened to Carl Trenholm, and a couple of wanted bank robbers drove through here fifteen or twenty minutes ago and I got to——"

I was back by the telephone by the time I'd said all that and I was reaching up for the receiver. But I never quite touched it.

A voice behind me said, "Take it easy, Buster."

CHAPTER SIX

"What matters it how far we go?" his scaly friend replied.
"There is another shore, you know, upon the other side.
The further off from England the nearer is to France –
Then turn not pale, beloved snail, but come and join the dance."

I TURNED around slowly. They'd been sitting at the table around the el of the tavern, the one table that can't be seen through the glass of the door or the windows. They'd probably picked it for that reason. The beer glasses in front of them were empty. But I didn't think the guns in their hands would be.

One of the guns—the one in the hand of Bat Masters' companion—was aimed at Smiley. And Smiley, not smiling, was keeping his hands very still, not moving a muscle.

The gun in Masters' hand was aimed at me.

He said, "So you knew us, huh, Buster?"

There wasn't any use denying it; I'd said too much already. I said, "You're Bat Masters." I looked at the other man, whom I hadn't seen clearly before, when he'd been in the car. He was squat and stocky, with a bullet head and little pig eyes. He looked like a caricature of a German army officer. I said, "I'm sorry; I don't know your friend."

Masters laughed. He said, "See, George, I'm famous and you're not. How'd you like that?"

George kept his eyes on Smiley. He said, "I think you better come around this side of the bar. You just might have a gun back there and take a notion to dive for it."

"Come on over and sit with us," Masters said. "Both of you. Let's make it a party, huh, George?"

George said, "Shut up," which changed my opinion of George quite a bit. I personally wouldn't have cared to tell Bat Masters to shut up, and in that tone of voice. True I *had* been fresh with him about twenty minutes before, but I hadn't known who he was. I hadn't even seen how big he was.

Smiley was coming around the end of the bar. I caught his eye, and gave him what was probably a pretty sickly grin. I said, "I'm sorry, Smiley. Looks like I put our foot in it this time."

His face was completely impassive. He said, "Not your fault, Doc."

I wasn't too sure of that myself. I was just remembering that I'd vaguely noticed a car parked in front of Smiley's place. If my brains had been in the proper end of my anatomy I'd have had the sense to take a quick look at that car. And if I'd had that much sense, I'd have had the further sense to go across to the *Clarion* office instead of barging nitwittedly into Smiley's and into the arms of Bat Masters and George.

And if the state police had come before they'd left Smiley's, the *Clarion* would have had a really good story. This way, it might be a good story too, but who would write it?

Smiley and I were standing close together now, and Masters must have figured that one gun was enough for both of us. He stuck his into a shoulder holster and looked at George. "Well?" he said.

That proved again that George was the boss, or at least was on equal status with Masters. And as I studied George's face, I could see why. Masters was big and probably had plenty of brass and courage, but George was the one of the two who had the more brains.

George said, "Guess we'll have to take 'em along, Bat."

I knew what that meant. I said, "Listen, there's a back room. Can't you just tie us up? If we're found a few hours from now, what does it matter? You'll be clear."

"And you might be found in a few minutes. And you probably noticed what kind of car we got, and you know which way we're heading." He shook his head, and it was definite.

He said, "We're not sticking around, either, till somebody comes in. Bat, go look outside."

Masters got up and started toward the front; then he hesitated and went back of the bar instead. He took two pint bottles of whisky and put one in either coat pocket. And he punched "No Sale" on the register and took out the bills; he didn't bother with the change. He folded the bills and stuck them in his trouser pocket. Then he came back around the bar and started for the door.

Sometimes I think people are crazy. Smiley stuck out his hand. He said, "Five bucks. Two-fifty apiece for those pints."

He could have got shot for it, then and there, but for some reason Masters liked it. He grinned and took the wadded paper out of his pocket, peeled a five loose and put it in Smiley's hand.

George said, "Bat, cut the horseplay. Look outside." I noticed that he watched very carefully and kept the gun trained smack in the middle of Smiley's chest while Smiley stuck the five-dollar bill into his pocket.

Masters opened the door and stepped outside, looked around casually and beckoned to us. Meanwhile George had stood up and walked around behind us, sliding his gun into a coat pocket out of sight but keeping his hand on it.

He said, "All right, boys, get going."

It was all very friendly. In a way.

We went out the door into the cool pleasant evening that wasn't going to last much longer, the way things looked now. Yes, the Buick was parked right in front of Smiley's. If I'd only glanced at it before I went in, the whole mess wouldn't have happened.

The Buick was a four-door sedan. George said, "Get in back," and we got in back. George got in front but sat sidewise, turned around facing us over the seat.

Masters got in behind the wheel and started the engine. He said over his shoulder, "Well, Buster, where to?"

I said, "About five miles out there are woods. If you take us back in them and tie us up, there isn't a chance on earth we'd be found before tomorrow."

I didn't want to die, and I didn't want Smiley to die, and that idea was such a good one that for a moment I hoped. Then Masters said, "What town is this, Buster?" and I knew there wasn't any chance. Just because I'd given him a fresh answer to a fresh question half an hour ago, there wasn't any chance.

The car pulled out from the kerb and headed north.

I was scared and sober. There didn't seem to be any reason why I had to be both. I said, "How about a drink?"

George reached into Masters' coat pocket and handed one of the pint bottles over the back of the seat. My hands shook a little while I got the cellophane off with my thumb nail and unscrewed the cap. I handed it to Smiley first and he took a short drink and passed it back. I took a long one and it put a warm spot where a very cold one had been. I don't meant to say it made me happy, but I felt a little better. I wondered what Smiley was thinking about and I remembered that he had a wife and three kids and I wished I hadn't remembered that.

I handed him back the bottle and he took another quick nip. I said, "I'm sorry, Smiley," and he said. "That's all right, Doc." And he laughed. "One bad thing, Doc. There'll be a swell story for your *Clarion*, but can Pete write it?"

I found myself wondering that, quite seriously. Pete's one of the best all-round printers in Illinois, but what kind of a job would he make of things tonight and tomorrow morning? He'd get the paper out all right, but he'd never done any news writing—at least as long as he'd worked for me—and handling all the news he was going to have tomorrow would be plenty tough. An escaped maniac, whatever had happened to Carl, and whatever—as if I really wondered—was going to happen to Smiley and me. I wondered if our bodies would be found in time to make the paper, or if it would be merely a double disappearance. We'd both be missed fairly soon. Smiley because his tavern was still open but no one behind the bar. I because I was due to meet Pete at the *Clarion* and about an hour from now, when I hadn't shown up yet, he'd start checking.

We were just leaving town by then, and I noticed that we'd got off the main street which was part of the main highway. Burgoyne Street, which we were on, was turning into a road.

Masters stopped the car as we came to a fork and turned around. "Where do these roads go?" he asked.

"They both go to Watertown," I told him. "The one to the left goes along the river and the other one cuts through the hills; it's shorter, but it's trickier driving."

Apparently Masters didn't mind tricky driving. He swung right and we started up into the hills. I wouldn't have done it myself, if I'd been driving. The hills are pretty hilly and the road through them is narrow and does plenty of winding, with a drop-off on one side or the other most of the time. Not the long precipitous drop-off you find on real mountain roads, but enough to wreck a car that goes over the edge, and enough to bother my touch of acrophobia.

Phobias are ridiculous things, past reasoning. I felt mine coming back the moment there was that slight drop-off at the side of the road as we started up the first hill. Actually, I was for the moment more afraid of that than of George's gun. Yes, phobias are funny things. Mine, fear of heights, is one of the commonest. Carl is afraid of cats. Al Grainger is a pyrophobiac, morbidly afraid of fire.

Smiley said, "You know, Doc?"

"What?" I asked him.

"I was thinking of Pete having to write that newspaper. Whyn't you come back and help him. Ain't there such things as ghost writers?"

I groaned. After all these years, Smiley had picked a time like this to come up with the only funny thing I'd ever heard him say.

We were up high now, about as high as the road went; ahead was a hairpin turn as it started downhill again. Masters stopped the car. "Okay, you mugs," he said. "Get out and start walking back."

Start, he'd said; he hadn't made any mention of finishing. The tail lights of the car would give them enough illumination to shoot us down by. And he'd probably picked this spot because it would be easy to roll our bodies off the edge of the road, down the slope, so they wouldn't be found right away. Both of them were already getting out of the car.

Smiley's big hand gave my arm a quick squeeze; I didn't know whether it was a farewell gesture or a signal. He said, "Go ahead, Doc," as calmly as though he was collecting for drinks back of his bar.

I opened the door on my side, but I was afraid to step out. Not because I knew I was going to be shot—that would happen anyway, even if I didn't get out. They'd either drag me out or else shoot me where I sat and bloody up the back seat of their car. No, I was afraid to get out because the car was on the outside edge of the road and the slope started only a yard from the open door of the car. My damned acrophobia. It was dark out there and I could see the edge of the road and no farther and I pictured a precipice beyond. I hesitated, half in the door and half out of it.

Smiley said again, "Go ahead, Doc," and I heard him moving behind me.

Then suddenly there was a click—and complete and utter darkness. Smiley had reached a long arm across the back of the seat to the dashboard and had turned the light switch off. All the car lights went out.

There was a shove in the middle of my back that sent me out of that car door like a cork popping out of a champagne bottle; I don't think my feet touched that yard-wide strip of road at all. As I went over the edge into darkness and the unknown I heard swearing and a shot behind me. I was so scared of falling that I'd gladly have been back up on the road trying to outrun a bullet back toward town. At least I'd have been dead before they rolled me over the edge.

I hit and fell and rolled. It wasn't really steep, after all; it was about a forty-five degree slope, and it was grassy. I flattened a couple of bushes before one stopped me. I could hear Smiley coming after me, sliding, and I scrambled on as fast as I could. All of my arms and legs seemed to be working, so I couldn't be seriously hurt.

And I could see a little now that my eyes were getting used to the darkness. I could see trees ahead, and I scrambled toward them down the slope, sometimes running, sometimes sliding and sometimes simply falling, which is the simplest if not the most comfortable way to go down a hill.

I made the trees, and heard Smiley make them, just as the lights of the car flashed on, on the road above us. Some shots snapped our way, and then I heard George say, "Don't waste it. Let's get going," and Bat's, "You mean we're gonna——"

George growled, "Hell, yes. That's woods down there. We could waste an hour playing hide and seek. Let's get going."

They were the sweetest words I'd heard in a long time.

I heard car doors slam, and the car started.

Smiley's voice, about two yards to my left, said, "Doc? You okay?"

"I think so," I said. "Smart work, Smiley, Thanks."

He came around a tree toward me and I could see him now. He said, "Save it, Doc. Come on quick. We got a chance—a little chance, anyway—of stopping them."

"Stopping them?" I said. My voice went shrill and sounded strange to me. I wondered if Smiley had gone crazy. I couldn't think of anything

in the whole wide world that I wanted to do less than stop Bat Masters and George.

But he had hold of my arm and was starting downhill, through the dimly seen trees and away from the road, taking me with him.

He said, "Listen, Doc, I know this country like the palm of my foot. I've hunted here often."

"For bank robbers?" I asked him.

"Listen, that road makes a hairpin and goes by right below us, not forty yards from here. If we can get just above the road before they get there and if I can find a big boulder to roll down as the car goes by——"

I wasn't crazy about it, but he was pulling me along and we were through the trees already. My eyes were used to the darkness by now and I could see the road dimly, a dozen yards ahead and a dozen yards below. In the distance, around a curve, I could hear the sound of the car; I couldn't see it yet. It was a long way off, but coming fast.

Smiley said, "Look for a boulder, Doc. If you don't find one big enough to roll, then something we can throw. If we can hit their windshield or something——"

He was bending over, groping around. I did the same, but the bank was smooth and grassy. If there were stones, I couldn't find any.

Apparently Smiley wasn't having any luck either. He swore. He said. "If I only had a gun——"

I remembered something. "I've got one," I said.

He straightened up and looked at me—and I'm glad it was dark enough that he couldn't see my face and that I couldn't see his.

I handed him the gun. The headlights of the car were coming in sight now around the curve. Smiley pushed me back into the trees and stood behind one himself, leaning out to expose only his head and his gun hand.

The car came like a bat out of hell, but Smiley took aim calmly. He fired his first shot when the car was about forty yards away, the second when it was only twenty. The first shot went into the radiator—I don't mean we could tell that then, but that's where it was found afterwards. The second went through the windshield, almost dead centre, but, of course, at an angle. It ploughed a furrow along the side of Masters' neck.

The car careened and then went off the road on the downhill side, away from us. It turned over once, end for end, the headlight beams stabbing the night with drunken arcs, and then it banged into a tree with a noise like the end of the world and stopped.

For just a second after all that noise there was a silence that was almost deafening. And then the gas tank exploded.

The car caught fire and there was plenty of light. We saw, as we ran toward it, that one of the men had been thrown clear; when we got close enough we could see that it was Masters. George was still in the car, but we couldn't do a thing for him. And in that roaring inferno there wasn't a chance on earth that he could have lived even the minute it took us to get to the scene of the wreck.

We dragged Masters farther away from the fire before we checked to see whether or not he was alive. Amazingly, he was. His face looked as though he'd held it in a meat grinder and both of his arms were broken. Whether there was anything wrong with him beyond that we couldn't tell, but he was still breathing and his heart was still beating.

Smiley was staring at the flaming wreck. He said, "A perfectly good Buick shot to hell. A fifty model at that." He shook his head sadly and then jumped back, as I did, when there was another explosion in the car; it must have been the cartridges in George's pistol going off all at once.

I told Smiley, "One of us will have to walk back. One had better stay here, on account of Masters' still being alive."

"I guess so," he said. "Don't know what either of us can do for him, but we can't both walk off and leave him. Say, look, that's a car coming."

I looked where he was pointing, toward the upper stretch of road where we'd got out of the car before it made the hairpin turn, and there were the headlights of a coming car all right.

We got out on the road ready to hail it, but it would have stopped anyway. It was a state police car with two coppers in it. Luckily, I knew one of them—Willie Feeble—and Smiley knew the other one, so they took our word for what had happened. Especially as Feeble knew about Masters and was able to identify him in spite of the way his face was cut up.

Masters was still alive and his heartbeat and breathing were as good as they'd been when we'd got to him. Feeble decided he'd better not try to move him. He went back to the police car and used the two-way radio to get an ambulance started our way and to report in to headquarters what had happened.

Feeble came back and said, "We'll give you and your friend a lift into town as soon as the ambulance gets here. You'll have to make and sign statements and stuff, but the chief says you can do that tomorrow; he knows both of you and says it's all right that way."

"That's swell," I said. "I've got to get back to the office as soon as I can. And as for Smiley here, his place is open and nobody there." I had a sudden thought and said, "Say, Smiley, you don't by any chance still have that pint that we had a nip out of in the car, do you?"

He shook his head. "What with turning off the lights and pushing you out and getting out myself——"

I sighed at the waste of good liquor. The other pint bottle, the one that had been in Bat Masters' left coat pocket, hadn't survived the crash. Still, Smiley *had* saved our lives, so I had to forgive him for abandoning the bottle he'd been holding.

The fire was dying down now, and I was getting a little sick at the barbecue odour and wished the ambulance would come so we could get away from here.

I suddenly remembered Carl and asked Feeble if there'd been any report on the police radio about a Carl Trenholm. He shook his head. He said, "There was a looney loose, though. Escaped from the county asylum. Must've been caught though; we had a cancellation on it later."

That was good news, in a way. It meant that Yehudi hadn't waited at my place after all. And somehow I'd hated the thought of having to put the guards on him while he was there. Insane or not, it didn't seem like real hospitality to a guest.

And the fact that nothing had been on the police radio about Carl at least wasn't discouraging.

A car came along from the opposite direction and stopped when its driver saw the smouldering wreckage and the state police car. It turned out to be a break for Smiley and me. The driver was a Watertown man whom Willie Feeble knew and who was on his way to Carmel City. When Feeble introduced us and vouched for us, he said he'd be glad to take Smiley and me into Carmel City with him.

I didn't believe it at first when I saw by the clock dial on the instrument panel of the car that it was only a few minutes after ten o'clock as we entered Carmel City; it seemed incredible that so much had happened in the few hours—less than four—since I'd left the *Clarion*. But we passed a lighted clock in a store window and I saw that the clock in the car was right after all, within a few minutes, anyway. It was only a quarter after ten.

We were let off in front of Smiley's. Across the street I could see lights were on at the *Clarion,* so Pete would be there. I thought I'd take a quick drink with Smiley, though, before I went to the office, so I went in with him.

The place was as we'd left it. If any customer had come in he'd got tired of waiting and had left.

Smiley went around back of the bar and poured us drinks while I went to the phone. I was going to call the hospital to find out about Carl Trenholm; then I decided to call Pete instead. He'd surely have called the hospital already. So I gave the *Clarion* number.

When Pete recognized my voice, he said, "Doc, where the hell have you been?"

"Tell you in a minute. Pete. First, have you got anything about Carl?"

"He's all right. I don't know yet what happened, but he's okay. I called the hospital and they said he'd been treated and released. I tried to find out what the injuries had been and how they'd happened, but they said they couldn't give out that information. I tried his home, but I guess he hadn't got there yet; nobody answered."

"Thanks, Pete," I said. "That's swell. Listen, there's going to be plenty to write up. Carl's accident, when we get in touch with him, and the escape and capture of the lunatic, and—something even bigger than either of those. So I guess we might as well do it tonight, if that's okay by you."

"Sure, Doc. I'd rather get it over with tonight. Where are you?"

"Over at Smiley's. Come on over for a quick one—to celebrate Carl's being okay. He can't even be badly hurt if they released him that quickly."

"Okay, Doc, I'll have one. But where were you? And Smiley, too, for that matter? I looked in there on my way to the office—saw the lights weren't on here, so I knew you weren't here yet—and you and Smiley were both gone. I waited five or ten minutes and then I decided I'd better come across here in case of any phone calls and to start melting metal in the Linotype."

I said, "Smiley and I had a little ride. I'll tell you about it."

"Okay, Doc. See you in a couple of minutes."

I went back to the bar and when I reached for the shot Smiley had poured for me, my hand was shaking.

Smiley grinned and said, "Me too, Doc." He held out his hand and I saw it wasn't much steadier than mine.

"Well," he said, "you got your story, Doc. What you were squawking about. Say, here's your gun back." He took out the short-barrelled thirty-eight and put it on the bar. "Good as new, except two bullets gone out of it. How'd' you happen to have it with you, Doc?"

For some reason I didn't want to tell him, or anyone, that the escaped lunatic had made such a sap out of me and had been a guest at my house. So I said, "I had to walk down here, and Pete had just phoned me there was a lunatic loose, so I stuck that in my pocket. Jittery, I guess."

He looked at me and shook his head slowly. I know he was thinking about my having had that gun in my pocket all along during what we thought was our last ride, and never having even tried to use it. I'd been so scared that I'd completely forgotten about it until Smiley had said he wished he had a gun.

I grinned and said, "Smiley, you're right in what you're thinking. I've got no more business with a gun than a snake has with roller skates. Keep it."

"Huh? You mean it, Doc? I've been thinking about getting one to keep under the bar."

"Sure, I mean it," I told him. "I'm afraid of the damn things and I'm safer without one."

He hefted it appraisingly. "Nice gun. It's worth something."

I said, "So's my life, Smiley. To me, anyway. And you saved it when you pushed me out of that car and over the edge tonight."

"Forget it, Doc. I couldn't have got out that door myself with you asleep in it. And getting out of the other side of the car wouldn't have been such a hot idea. Well, if you really mean it, thanks for the gun."

He put it out of sight under the bar and then poured us each a second drink. "Make it short," I told him. "I've got a lot of work to do."

He glanced at his clock and it was only ten-thirty. He said, "Hell, Doc, the evening's only a pup."

I thought, but didn't say, *what a pup!*

I wonder what I'd have thought if I'd even guessed that the pup hadn't even been weaned yet.

Pete came in.

CHAPTER SEVEN

"It seems a shame," the Walrus said,
"To play them such a trick,
After we've brought them out so far,
And made them trot so quick!"

NEITHER Smiley nor I had touched, as yet, the second drink he'd poured us, so there was time for Pete Corey to get in on the round; Smiley poured a drink for him.

He said, "Okay, Doc, now what's this gag about Smiley and you going for a ride? You told me your car was laid up and Smiley doesn't drive one."

"Pete," I said, "Smiley doesn't *have* to be able to drive a car. He's a gentleman of genius. He kills or captures killers. That's what we were doing. Anyway, that's what Smiley was doing. I went along, just for the ride."

"Doc, you're kidding me."

I said, "If you don't believe me, read tomorrow's *Clarion*. Ever heard of Bat Masters?"

Pete shook his head. He reached for his drink.

"You will," I told him. "In tomorrow's *Clarion*. Ever heard of George?"

"George Who?"

I opened my mouth to say I didn't know, but Smiley beat me to the punch by saying, "George Kramer."

I stared at Smiley. "How'd you know his last name?"

"Saw it in a fact detective magazine. And his picture, too, and Bat Masters'. They're members of the Gene Kelley mob."

I stared harder at Smiley. "You recognized them? I mean, before I even came in here?"

"Sure," Smiley said. "But it wouldn't have been a good idea to phone the cops while they were here, so I was going to wait till they left, and then phone the state cops to pick 'em up between here and Chicago. That's where they were heading. I listened to what they said, and it wasn't much, but I did get that much out of it. Chicago. They had a date there tomorrow afternoon."

"You're not kidding, Smiley?" I asked him. "You really had them spotted before I came in here?"

"I'll show you the magazine, Doc, with their pictures in it. Pictures of all the Gene Kelley mob."

"Why didn't you tell me?"

Smiley shrugged his big shoulders. "You didn't ask. Why didn't you tell *me* you had a gun in your pocket? If you coulda slipped it to me in the car, we'd have polished 'em off sooner. It would have been a cinch; it was so dark in that back seat after we got out of town, George Kramer wouldn't of seen you pass it."

He laughed as though he'd said something funny. Maybe he had.

Pete was looking from one to the other of us. He said, "Listen, if this is a gag, you guys are going a long way for it. What the hell happened?"

Neither of us paid any attention to Pete. I said, "Smiley, where is that fact detective magazine? Can you get it?"

"Sure, it's upstairs. Why? Don't you believe me?"

"Smiley," I said. "I'd believe you if you told me you were lying. No, what I had in mind is that that magazine will save me a lot of grief. It'll have background stuff on the boys we were playing cops and robbers with tonight. I thought I'd have to phone to Chicago and get it from cops there. But if there's a whole article on the Gene Kelley mob in that mag, I'll have enough without that."

"Get it right away, Doc." Smiley went through the door that led upstairs.

I took pity on Pete and gave him a quick sketch of our experience with the gangsters. It was fun to watch his mouth drop open and to think that a lot of other mouths in Carmel City would do that same thing tomorrow when the *Clarion* was distributed.

Smiley came back down with the magazine and I put it in my pocket and went to the phone again. I still had to have the details about what had happened to Carl, for the paper. I still wanted it for my own information too, but that wasn't so important as long as he wasn't seriously hurt.

I tried the hospital first but they gave me the same runaround they'd given Pete; sorry, but since Mr. Trenholm had been discharged, they could give out no information. I thanked them. I tried Carl's own phone and got no answer, so I went back to Pete and Smiley.

Smiley happened to be staring out the window. He said, "Somebody just went in your office, Doc. Looked like Clyde Andrews."

Pete turned to look, too, but was too late. He said, "Guess that's who it must've been. Forgot to tell you, Doc; he phoned about twenty minutes ago while I was waiting for you over at the office. I told him I expected you any minute."

"You didn't lock the door, did you, Pete?" I asked. He shook his head.

I waited a minute to give the banker time to get up the stairs and into the office and then I went back to the phone and called the *Clarion* number. It rang several times while Clyde, apparently, was making up his mind whether to answer it or not. Finally he did.

"This is Doc, Clyde," I said. "How's the boy?"

"He's all right, Doc. He's fine. And I want to thank you again for what you did and—I want to talk to you about something. Are you on your way here?"

"I'm across the street at Smiley's. How about dropping over here if you want to talk?"

He hesitated. "Can't you come here?" he asked.

I grinned to myself. Clyde Andrews is not only a strict temperance advocate; he's head of a local chapter (a small one, thank God) of the Anti-Saloon League. He'd probably never been in a tavern in his life.

I said, "I'm afraid I can't, Clyde." I made my voice very grave. "I'm afraid if you want to talk to me, it will have to be here at Smiley's."

He got me, all right. He said stiffly, "I'll be there."

I sauntered back to the bar. I said, "Clyde Andrews is coming here, Smiley. Chalk up a first."

Smiley stared at me. "I don't believe it," he said. He laughed.

"Watch," I told him.

Solemnly I went around behind the bar and got a bottle and two glasses and took them to a table—the one in the far corner farthest from the bar. I liked the way Pete and Smiley stared at me.

I filled both the glasses and sat down. Pete and Smiley stared some more. Then they turned and stared the other way as Clyde came in, walking stiffly. He said, "Good evening, Mr. Corey," to Pete and "Good evening, Mr. Wheeler" to Smiley, and then came back to where I was sitting.

I said, "Sit down Clyde," and he sat down.

I looked at him. I said sternly, "Clyde, I don't like—in advance—what you're going to ask me."

"But, Doc," he said earnestly, almost pleadingly, *"must* you print what happened? Harvey didn't mean to———"

"That's what I meant," I said. "What makes you think I'd even think of printing a word about it?"

He looked at me and his face changed. "Doc! You're not going to?"

"Of course not." I leaned forward. "Listen, Clyde, I'll make you a bet—or I would if you were a betting man. I'll bet I know exactly the amount of money the kid had in his pocket when he was leaving—and, no, I didn't look in his pockets. I'll bet he had a savings account—he's been working summers several years now, hasn't he?—and he was running away. And he knew damn well you wouldn't let him draw his own money and that he couldn't draw it without your knowing it. Whether he had twenty dollars or a thousand, I'll bet you it was the exact amount of his own account."

He took a deep breath. "You're right. Exactly right. And—thanks for thinking that, before you knew it. I was going to tell you."

"For a fifteen-year-old, Harvey's a good kid, Clyde. Now listen, you'll admit I did the right thing tonight calling you instead of calling the sheriff? And in keeping the story out of the paper?"

"Yes."

"You're in a saloon, Clyde. A den of iniquity. You should have said, 'Hell, yes.' But I don't suppose it would sound natural if you did, so I won't insist on it. But, Clyde, how much thinking have you been doing about *why* the boy was running away? Has he told you that yet?"

He shook his head slowly. "He's all right now, in bed, asleep. Dr. Minton gave him a sedative, but told me Harvey had better not do any talking till tomorrow."

"I'll tell you right now," I said, "that he won't have any very coherent story about it. Maybe he'll say he was running away to join the army or to go on the stage or—or almost anything. But it won't be the truth, even if he thinks it is. Clyde, whether he knows it or not, he was running *away*. Not toward."

"Away from what?"

"From you," I said.

For a second I thought he was going to get angry and I'm glad he didn't, because then I might have got angry too and that would have spoiled the whole thing.

Instead, he slumped a little. He said, "Go on, Doc."

I hated to, then, but I had to strike while the striking was good. I said, "Listen, Clyde, get up and walk out any time you want to; I'm going to give it to you straight. You've been a lousy father." At any other time he'd have walked out on me on that one. I could tell by his face that, even now, he didn't like it. But at any other time he wouldn't have been sitting at a back table in Smiley's tavern, either.

I said, "You're a good man, Clyde, but you work at it too hard. You're rigid, unyielding, righteous. Nobody can love a ramrod. There's nothing wrong with your being religious, if you want to. Some men *are* religious. But you've got to realize that everybody who doesn't think as you do isn't necessarily wrong."

I said, "Take alcohol—literally, if you wish; there's a glass of whisky in front of you. But take it figuratively, anyway. It's been a solace to the human race, one of the things that can make life tolerable, since—damn it, since before the human race was even human. True, there are a few people who can't handle it—but that's no reason to try to legislate it away from the people who *can* handle it, and whose enjoyment of life is increased by its moderate use—or even by its occasional immoderate use, providing it doesn't make them pugnacious or otherwise objectionable.

"But—let's skip alcohol. My point is that a man can be a good man without trying to interfere with his neighbour's life too much. Or with his son's. Boys are human, Clyde. People in general are human; people are more human than anybody."

He didn't say anything, and that was a hopeful sign. Maybe a tenth of it was sinking in.

I said, "Tomorrow, when you can talk with the kid, Clyde, what are you going to say?"

"I—I don't know, Doc."

I said, "Don't say anything. Above all, don't ask him any questions. Not a damn question. And let him keep that money, in cash, so he can run away any time he decides to. Then maybe he won't. If you change your attitude toward him.

"But, damn it, Clyde, you *can't* change your attitude toward him, and unbend, without unbending in general toward the human race. The kid's a human being, too. And you could be, if you wanted to. Maybe you think it will cost you your immortal soul to be one—I don't think so, myself, and I think there are a great many truly religious people who don't think so either—but if you persist in not being one, then you're going to lose your son."

I decided that that was it. There wasn't anything more that I could say that couldn't weaken my case. I decided I'd better shut up. I did shut up.

It seemed like a long, long time before he said anything. He was staring at the wall over my head. When he answered what I'd said, he still didn't say anything. He did better, a lot better.

He picked up the whisky in front of him. I got mine picked up in time to down it as he took a sip of his. He made a face.

"Tastes horrible," he said. "Doc, do you really *like* this stuff?"

"No," I told him. "I hate the taste of it. You're right, Clyde, it *is* horrible."

He looked at the glass in his hand and shuddered a little. I said, "Don't drink it. That sip you took proved your point. And don't try to toss it off; you'll probably choke."

He said, "I suppose you have to learn to like it. Doc, I've drunk a little wine a few times, not recently, but I didn't dislike it too much. Does Mr. Wheeler have any wine?"

"The name is Smiley," I said, "and he does." I stood up. I clapped him on the back, and it was the first time in my life I'd ever done so.

I said, "Come on, Clyde, let's see what the boys in the back room will have."

I took him over to the bar, to Pete and Smiley. I told Smiley, "We want a round, and it's on Clyde. Wine for him, and I'll take a short beer this time; I've got to rewrite a paper tonight."

I frowned at Smiley because of the utterly amazed look on his face, and he got the hint and straightened it out. He said, "Sure, Mr. Andrews. What kind of wine?"

"Do you have sherry, Mr. Wheeler?"

I said, "Clyde, meet Smiley. Smiley, Clyde."

Smiley laughed, and Clyde smiled. The smile was a bit stiff, and would take practice, but I knew and knew damned well that Harvey Andrews wasn't going to run away from home again.

He was going, henceforth, to have a father who was human. Oh, I don't mean that I expected Clyde suddenly to turn into Smiley's best customer. Maybe he'd never come back to Smiley's again. But by ordering one drink—even of wine—across a bar, he'd crossed a Rubicon. He wasn't perfect any more.

I was beginning to feel my own drinks again and I didn't really want the one Clyde bought for me, but it was an Occasion, so I took it. But I was getting in a hurry to get back across the street to the *Clarion* and get to work on all the stories I had to write, so I downed it fairly quickly and Pete and I left. Clyde left when we did, because he wanted to get back to his son; I didn't blame him for that.

At the *Clarion*, Pete checked the pot on the Linotype—and found it hot enough—while I pulled up the typewriter stand beside my desk and started abusing the ancient Underwood. I figured that, with the dope in the fact detective magazine Smiley had given me for background, I could run it to three or four columns, so I had a lot of work ahead of me. The escaped looney and Carl could wait—now that the former was captured and now that I knew Carl was safe—until I got the main story done.

I told Pete, while he was waiting for the first take, to hand set a banner head, "TAVERNKEEPER CAPTURES WANTED KILLERS," to see if it would fit. Oh, sure, I was going to put myself in the story, too, but I was going to make Smiley the hero of it, for one simple reason. He had been.

Pete had the head set up—and it fitted—by the time I had a take for him to start setting on the machine.

In the middle of the second take I realized that I didn't know for sure that Bat Masters was still alive, although I'd put it that way in the lead. I might as well find out for sure that he really was, and what condition he was in.

I knew better than to call the hospital for anything more detailed than whether he was dead or not, so I picked up the phone and called the state police office at Watertown. Willie Feeble answered.

He said, "Sure, Doc, he's alive. He's even been conscious and talked some. Thinks he's dying, so he really opened up."

"Is he dying?"

"Sure, but not the way he thinks. It'll cost the state some kilowatts. And he can't beat the rap; they've got the whole gang cold, once they catch them. There were six people—two of 'em women—killed in that bank job they pulled at Colby."

"Was George in on that?"

"Sure. He was the one that shot the women. One was a teller and the other one was a customer who was too scared to move when they told her to lie flat."

That made me feel a little better about what had happened to George. Not that it had worried me too much.

I said, "Then I can put in the story that Bat Masters confesses?"

"I dunno about that, Doc. Captain Evans is at the hospital talking to him now, and we had one report here that Masters is talking, but not the details. I don't think the cap would even bother asking him about that stuff."

"What would he ask him, then?"

"The rest of the mob, where they are There are two others besides Gene Kelley, and it'd be a real break if the cap can get out of Masters something that would help us find the others. Especially Kelley. The two we got tonight are peanuts compared to Kelley."

I said, "Thanks a lot, Willie. Listen, if anything more breaks on the story, will you give me a ring? I'll be here at the *Clarion* for a while yet."

"Sure," he said. "So long."

74

I hung up and went back to the story. It went sweetly. I was on the fourth take when the phone rang and it was Captain Evans of the state police, calling from the hospital where they'd taken Masters. He'd just phoned Watertown and knew about my call there.

He said, "Mr. Stoeger? You going to be there another fifteen or twenty minutes?"

I was probably going to be working another several hours, I told him.

"Fine," he said, "I'll drive right around."

That was duck soup; I'd have my story about his questioning Masters right from the horse's mouth. So I didn't bother asking him any questions over the phone.

And I found myself, when I'd finished that take, up to the point in the story where the questioning of Masters should come, so I decided I might as well wait until I'd talked to Evans, since he was going to be here so soon.

Meanwhile I might as well start checking on the other two stories again. I called Carl Trenholm, still got no answer. I called the county asylum.

Dr. Buchan, the superintendent, wasn't there, the girl at the switchboard told me; she asked if I wanted to talk to his assistant and I said yes.

She put him on and before I'd finished explaining who I was and what I wanted, he'd interrupted me. "He's on his way over to see you now, Mr. Stoeger. You're at the *Clarion* office?"

"Yes," I said, "I'm here now. And you say Dr. Buchan's on his way? That's fine."

My stories were coming to me, I thought happily, as I put the phone back. Both Captain Evans and Dr. Buchan. Now if only Carl would drop in too and explain what had happened to him.

He did. Not that exact second, but only about two minutes later. I'd wandered over to the stone and was looking gloatingly at the horrible front page with no news on it and thinking how lovely it was going to look a couple of hours from now and listening with pleasure to the click of the mats down the channels of the Linotype, when the door opened and Carl walked in.

His clothes were a little dusty and dishevelled; he had a big patch of adhesive tape on his forehead and his eyes looked a little bleary. He had a sheepish grin.

He said, "Hi, Doc. How's everything?"

"Wonderful," I told him. "What happened to you Carl?"

"That's what I dropped in to tell you, Doc. Thought you might get a garbled version of it and be worried about me."

"I couldn't even get a garbled version. No version at all; the hospital wouldn't give. What happened?"

"Got drunk. Went for a walk out the pike to sober up and got so woozy I had to lie down a minute, so I headed for the grassy strip the other side of the ditch alongside the road and—well, my foot slipped as I was stepping across the ditch and the ground, with a chunk of rock in its hand, reached up and slapped me in the face."

"Who found you, Carl?" I asked him.

He chuckled. "I don't even know. I woke up—or came to—in the sheriff's car on the way to the hospital. Tried to talk him out of taking me there, but he insisted. They checked me for a concussion and let me go."

"How do you feel now?"

"Do you really want to know?"

"Well," I said, "maybe not. Want a drink?"

He shuddered. I didn't insist. Instead, I asked him where he'd been since he'd left the hospital.

"Drinking black coffee at the Greasy Spoon. Think I'm able to make it home by now. In fact, I'm on my way. But I knew you'd have heard about it and thought you might as well have the—uh—facts straight in case—uh——"

"Don't be an ass, Carl," I told him. "You don't rate a stick of type, even if you wanted it. And, by the way, Smiley gave me the inside dope on Bonney's divorce, so I cut down the story to essentials and cut out the charges against Bonney."

"That's swell of you, Doc."

"Why didn't you tell me the truth about it yourself?" I asked him. "Afraid of interfering with the freedom of the press? Or of taking advantage of a friendship?"

"Well—somewhere in between, I guess. Anyway, thanks. Well, maybe I'll see you tomorrow. If I live that long."

He left and I wandered back to my desk. The Linotype was caught up to the typewriter by now, and I hoped Evans would show up soon—or Dr. Buchan from the asylum—so I could get ahead with at least one of the stories and not keep Pete working any later than necessary. For myself, I didn't give a damn. I was too keyed up to have been able to sleep anyway.

Well, there was one thing we could be doing to save time later. We went over to the stone and started pulling all the filler items out of the back pages so we could move back the least important stories on page one to make room for the two big stories we still had coming. We'd need at least two full page one columns—and more if we could manage it—for the capture of the bank robbers and the escape of the maniac.

We were just getting the pages unlocked, though, when Dr. Buchan came in. An elderly lady—she looked vaguely familiar to me, but I couldn't place her—was with him.

She smiled at me and said. "Do you remember me, Mr. Stoeger?" And the smile did it; I did remember her. She'd lived next door to me when I was a kid, forty-some years ago, and she'd given me cookies. And I remembered now that, while I was away at college, I'd heard that she had gone mildly, not dangerously, insane and had been taken to the asylum. That must have been—Good Lord—thirty-some years ago. She must be well over seventy by now. And her name was——

"Certainly, Mrs. Griswald," I told her. "I even remember the cookies and candy you used to give me."

And I smiled back at her. She looked so happy that one couldn't help smiling back at her.

She said, "I'm so glad you remember, Mr. Stoeger. I want you to do me a big favour—and I'm so glad you remember those days, because maybe you'll do it for me. Dr. Buchan—he's so wonderful—offered to bring me here so I could ask you. I—I really wasn't running away this evening. I was just confused. The door was open and I forgot. I was thinking that it was forty years ago and I wondered what I was doing there and why I wasn't home with Otto, and so I just started home, that's all. And by the time I remembered that Otto was dead for so long and that I was——"

The smile was tremulous now, and there were tears in her eyes. "Well, by that time I was lost and couldn't find my way back, until they found me. I even—*tried* to find my way back, once I remembered and knew where I was supposed to be."

I glanced over her head at tall Dr. Buchan and he nodded to me. But I still didn't know what it was all about. I didn't see, so I said, "I see, Mrs. Griswald."

Her smile was back. She nodded brightly. "Then you *won't* put it in the paper? About my wandering away, I mean? Because I didn't really mean to do it. And Clara, my daughter, lives in Springfield now, but she still subscribes to your paper for news from home, and if she reads in the *Clarion* that I—escaped—she'll think I'm not happy there and it'll worry her. And I *am* happy, Mr. Stoeger—Dr. Buchan is wonderful to me—and I don't want to make Clara unhappy or have her worry about me, and— you won't write it up, will you?"

I patted her shoulder gently. I said, "Of course not, Mrs. Griswald."

And then suddenly she was against my chest, crying, and I was embarrassed as hell. Until Dr. Buchan pulled her gently away and started her toward the door. He stepped back a second and said to me so quietly that she couldn't hear, "It's straight, Stoeger. I mean, it probably would worry her daughter a lot and she really wasn't escaping—she just wandered off. And her daughter really does read your paper."

"Don't worry," I said. "I won't mention it."

Past him, I could see the door open and Captain Evans of the state police was coming in. He left the door open and Mrs. Griswald was wandering through it.

Dr. Buchan shook hands quickly. He said, "Thanks a lot, then. And on my behalf as well as Mrs. Griswald's. It doesn't do an institution like ours any good to have publicity on escapes, of course. Not that I'd have asked you, myself, to suppress the story on that account. But since our patient had a really good, legitimate, reason to ask you not to——"

He happened to turn and see that his patient was already heading down the stairs. He hurried after her before she could again become confused and wander into limbo.

Another story gone, I thought, as I shook hands with Evans. Those cookies had been expensive—if worth it. I thought, suddenly, of all the stories I'd had to kill tonight. The bank burglary—for good and obvious reasons. Carl's accident—because it had been trivial after all, and writing it up would have hurt his reputation as a lawyer. The accident in the Roman candle department, because it might have lost Mrs. Carr's husband a needed job. Ralph Bonney's divorce—well, not killed, exactly, but played down from a long, important story to a short news item. Mrs. Griswald's escape from the asylum—because she'd given me cookies once and because it would have worried her daughter. Even the auction sale at the Baptist Church—for the most obvious reason of all, that it had been called off.

But what the hell did any of that matter as long as I had one really big story left, the biggest of them all? And there wasn't any conceivable reason why I couldn't print that one.

Captain Evans took the seat I pulled up for him by my desk and I sank back into the swivel chair and got a pencil ready for what he was going to tell me.

"Thanks a hell of a lot for coming here, Cap. Now what's the score about what you got out of Masters?"

He pushed his hat back on his head and frowned. He said, "I'm sorry, Doc. I'm going to have to ask you—on orders from the top—not to run the story at all."

CHAPTER EIGHT

He took his vorpal sword in hand:
Long time the manxome foe he sought—
So rested he by the Tumtum tree,
And stood awhile in thought.

I DON'T know what my face looked like. I know I dropped the pencil and that I had to clear my throat when what I started to say wouldn't come out the first time.

The second time, it came out, if a bit querulously. "Cap, you're kidding me. You can't really mean it. The one big thing that's ever happened here—Is this a gag?"

He shook his head. "Nope, Doc. It's the McCoy. It comes right from the chief himself. I can't *make* you hold back the story, naturally. But I want to tell you the facts and I hope you'll decide to."

I breathed a little more freely when he said he couldn't make me hold it back. It wouldn't hurt me to listen, politely.

"Go ahead," I told him. "It had better be good."

He leaned forward. "It's this way, Doc. This Gene Kelley mob is nasty stuff. Real killers. I guess you found that out tonight about two of them. And, by the way, you did a damn good job."

"Smiley Wheeler did. I just went along for the ride."

It was a weak joke, but he laughed at it. Probably just to please me. He said, "If we can keep it quiet for about forty more hours—till Saturday afternoon—we can break up the gang completely. Including the big shot himself, Gene Kelley."

"Why Saturday afternoon?"

"Masters and Kramer had a date for Saturday afternoon with Kelley and the rest of the mob. At a hotel in Gary, Indiana. They've been separated since their last job, and they'd arranged that date to get together for the next one, see? When Kelley and the others show up for that date, well, we've got 'em.

"That is, unless the news gets out that Masters and Kramer are already in the bag. Then Kelley and company won't show up."

"Why can't we twist one little thing in the story," I suggested. "Just say Masters and Kramer were both dead?"

He shook his head. "The other boys wouldn't take any chances. Nope, if they know our two boys were either caught or killed, they'll stay away from Gary in droves."

I sighed. I knew it wouldn't work, but I said hopefully, "Maybe none of the gang members reads the *Carmel City Clarion.*"

"You know better than that, Doc. Other papers all over the country would pick it up. The Saturday morning papers would have it, even if the Friday evening editions didn't get it." He had a sudden thought and looked startled. "Say, Doc, who represents the news services here? Have they got the story yet?"

"I represent them," I said sadly. "But I hadn't wired either of them on this yet. I was going to wait till my own paper was out. They'd have fired me, sure, and it would have cost me a few bucks a year, but for once I was going to have a big story break in my own paper before I threw it to the wolves."

He said, "I'm sorry, Doc. I guess this is a big thing for you. But now, at least, you won't lose out with the news services. You can say you held the story at the request of the police—until, say, mid-afternoon Saturday. Then send it in to them and get credit for it."

"Cash, you mean. I want the credit of breaking it in the *Clarion,* damn it."

"But will you hold it up, Doc? Listen, those boys are *killers.* You'll be saving lives if you let us get them. Do you know anything about Gene Kelley?"

I nodded; I'd been reading about him in the magazine Smiley had lent me. He wasn't a very nice man. Evans was right in saying it would cost human lives to print that story if the story kept Kelley out of the trap he'd otherwise walk into.

I looked up and Pete was standing there listening. I tried to judge from his face what he thought about it, but he was keeping it carefully blank.

I scowled at him and said, "Shut off that God damn Linotype. I can't hear myself think."

He went and shut it off.

Evans looked relieved. He said, "Thanks, Doc." For no reason at all—the evening was moderately cool—he pulled out a handkerchief and wiped his forehead. "What a break it was that Masters hated the rest of the mob enough to turn them in for us when he figured he was done himself. And that you're willing to hold the story till we get 'em. Well, you can use it next week."

There wasn't any use telling him that I could also print a chapter or two of Caesar's *Gallic Wars* next week; it was ancient history too.

So I didn't say anything and after a few more seconds he got up and left.

It seemed awfully quiet without the Linotype running. Pete came over. He said, "Well, Doc, we still got that nine-inch hole in the front page that you said you'd find some way of filling in the morning. Maybe while we're here anyway——"

I ran my fingers through what is left of my hair. "Run it as it is, Pete," I told him, "except with a black border around it."

"Look, Doc, I can pull forward that story on the Ladies' Aid election and if I reset it narrow measure to fit a box, it'll maybe run long enough."

I couldn't think of anything better. I said, "Sure, Pete," but when he started toward the Linotype to turn it back on, I said, "But not tonight, Pete. In the morning. It's half-past eleven. Get home to the wife and kiddies."

"But I'd just as soon——"

"Get the hell out of here," I said, "before I bust out blubbering. I don't want anybody to see me do it."

He grinned to show he knew I didn't really mean it and said, "Sure, Doc. I'll get down a little early, then. Seven-thirty. You going to stick around a while now?"

"A few minutes," I said, "'Night, Pete. Thanks for coming down, and everything."

I kept sitting at my desk for a minute after he'd left, and I didn't blubber, but I wanted to all right. It didn't seem possible that so much had happened and that I couldn't get even a stick of type out of any of it. For a few minutes I wished that I was a son-of-a-bitch instead of a sucker so I could go ahead and print it all. Even if it let the Kelley mob get away to do more killing, lost my housekeeper's husband her job, made a fool out of Carl Trenholm, worried Mrs. Griswald's daughter and ruined Harvey Andrew's reputation by telling how he'd been caught robbing his father's bank while running away from home. And while I was at it, I might as well smear Ralph Bonney by listing the untrue charges brought against him in the divorce case and write a humorous little item about the leader of the local antisaloon faction setting up a round for the boys at Smiley's. And even run the rummage sale story on the grounds that the cancellation had been too late and let a few dozen citizens make a trip in vain. It would be wonderful to be a son-of-a-bitch instead of a sucker so I could do all that. Sons-of-bitches must have more fun than people. And definitely they get out bigger and better newspapers.

I wandered over and looked at the front page lying there on the stone, and for something to do I dropped the filler items back in page four. The ones we'd taken out to let us move back the present junk from page one to make room for all the big stories we were going to break. I locked up the page again.

It was quiet as hell.

I wondered why I didn't get out of there and have another drink—or a hell of a lot of drinks—at Smiley's. I wondered why I didn't want to get stinking drunk. But I didn't.

I wandered over to the window and stood staring down at the quiet street. They hadn't rolled the sidewalks in yet—closing time for taverns is midnight in Carmel City—but nobody was walking on them.

A car went by and I recognized it as Ralph Bonney's car, heading probably to pick up Miles Harrison and take him over to Neilsville to pick up the night side pay roll for the fireworks plant, including the Roman candle department. To which I had briefly——

I decided I'd smoke one more cigarette and then go home. I reached into my pocket and pulled out the cigarette package and something fluttered to the floor—a card.

I picked it up and stared at it. It read:

Yehudi Smith

Suddenly the dead night was alive again. I'd written off Yehudi Smith when I'd heard that the escaped lunatic had been captured. I'd written him off so completely that I'd forgotten to write him on again when Dr. Buchan had brought in Mrs. Griswald to talk to me.

Yehudi Smith *wasn't* the escaped lunatic.

Suddenly I wanted to jump into the air and click my heels together, I wanted to run, I wanted to tell.

Then I remembered how long I'd been gone and I almost ran to the telephone on my desk. I gave my own number and my heart sank as it rang once, twice, thrice—and then after the fourth ring Smith's voice answered with a sleepy-sounding hello.

I said, "This is Doc Stoeger, Mr. Smith. I'm starting home now. Want to apologize for having kept you waiting so long. Some things happened."

"Good. I mean, good that you're coming now. What time is it?"

"About half-past eleven. I'll be there in fifteen minutes. And thanks for waiting."

I hurried into my coat and grabbed my hat. I almost forgot to turn out the lights and lock the door.

Smiley's first, but not for a drink; I picked up a bottle to take along. The one at my house had been getting low when I left; only God knew what had happened to it since.

Leaving Smiley's with the bottle, I swore again at the fact that my car was laid up with those flat tyres. Not that it's a long walk or that I mind walking in the slightest when I'm not in a hurry, but again I was in a hurry. Last time it had been because I thought Carl Trenholm was dead or seriously injured—and to get away from Yehudi Smith. This time it was to get back to him.

Past the post office, now dark. The bank, this time with the night light on and no evidence of crime in sight. Past the spot where the Buick had pulled up and a voice had asked someone named Buster what town this was. There wasn't a car in sight now, friend or foe. Past everything that I'd passed so many thousand times, and off the main street into the friendly, pleasant side streets no longer infested with homicidal maniacs or other horrors. I didn't look behind me once, all the way home.

I felt so good I felt silly. Best of all I was cold-sobered by everything that had been happening, and I was ready and in the mood for a few more drinks and some more screwy conversation.

I still didn't completely believe he'd be there, but he was.

And he looked so familiar sitting there that I wondered why I'd doubted. I said "Hi", and shied my hat at the hat-rack and it hit a peg and stayed there. It was the first time that had happened in months so I knew from that I was lucky tonight. As if I needed that to prove it.

I took the seat across from him, just as we'd been sitting before, and I poured us each a drink—still from the first bottle; apparently he hadn't drunk much while I'd been gone—and started to renew the apologies I'd made over the phone for having been away so long.

He waved the apologies away with a casual gesture. "It doesn't matter at all, as long as you got back." He smiled. "I had a nice nap."

We touched glasses and drank. He said, "Let's see; just where were we when you got that phone call—oh, which reminds me; you said it was about an accident to a friend. May I ask——?"

"He's all right," I told him. "Nothing serious. It was—well, other things kept coming up that kept me away so long."

"Good. Then—oh, yes, I remember. When the phone rang we were talking about the Roman candle department. We'd just drunk to it."

I remembered and nodded. "That's where I've been, ever since I left here."

"Seriously?"

"Quite," I said. "They fired me half an hour ago, but it was fun while it lasted. Wait; no, it wasn't. I won't lie to you. At the time it was happening, it was pretty horrible."

His eyebrows went up a little. "Then you're serious. Something did happen. You know, Doctor——"

"Doc," I said.

"You know, Doc, you're different. Changed, somehow."

I refilled our glasses, still from the first bottle, although that round killed it.

"It's temporary, I think. Yes, Mr. Smith, I had——"

"Smitty," he said.

"Yes, Smitty. I had a rather bad experience, while it lasted, and I'm still in reaction from it, but the reaction won't last. I'm still jittery from it and I may be even more jittery tomorrow when I realize what a narrow squeak I had, but I'm still the same guy; Doc Stoeger, fifty-three, genial failure both as a hero and as an editor."

Silence for a few seconds and then he said, "Doc, I like you. I think you're a swell guy. I don't know what happened, and I don't suppose you want to tell me, but I'll bet you one thing."

"Thanks, Smitty," I said. "And it's not that I don't want to tell you what happened this evening; it's just that I don't want to talk about it at all, right now. Some other time I'll be glad to tell you, but right now I want to stop thinking about it—and start thinking about Lewis Carroll again. What's the one thing you want to bet me, though?"

"That you're not a failure as an editor. As a hero, maybe—damned few of us are heroes. But I'll bet you said you were a failure as an editor because you killed a story—for some good reason. And not a selfish one. Would I win that bet?"

"You would," I said. I didn't tell him he'd have won it five times over. "But I'm not proud of myself—the only thing is that I'd have been ashamed of myself otherwise. This way, I'm going to be ashamed of my paper. All newspapermen, Smitty, should be sons-of-bitches."

"Why?" And before I could answer he tossed off the drink I'd just poured him—tossed it off as before with that fascinating trick of the glass never really nearing his lips—and answered it himself with a more unanswerable question. "So that newspapers will be more entertaining?—at the expense of human lives they might wreck or even destroy?"

The mood was gone, or the mood was wrong. I shook myself a little. I said, "Let's get back to Jabberwocks. And—My God, every time I get to talking seriously it sobers me up. I had such a nice edge early in the evening. Let's have another—and to Lewis Carroll again. And then go back to the gobbledegook you were giving me, the stuff that sounded like Einstein on a binge."

He grinned. "Wonderful word, gobbledegook. Carroll might have originated it, except that there was less of it in his time. All right, Doc, to Carroll."

And again his glass was empty. It was a trick I'd *have* to learn, no matter how much time it took or how much whisky it wasted. But, the first time, in private.

I drank mine and it was the third since I'd come home, fifteen minutes ago; I was beginning to feel them. Not that I feel three drinks starting from scratch, but these didn't start from scratch. I'd had quite a few early in the evening, before the fresh air of my little ride with Bat and George had cleared my head, and several at Smiley's thereafter.

They were hitting me now. Not hard, but definitely.

There was a mistiness about the room. We were talking about Carroll and mathematics again, or Yehudi Smith was talking, anyway, and I was trying to concentrate on what he saying. He seemed, for a moment, to blur a little and to advance and recede as I looked at him. And his voice was a blur, too, a blur of sines and cosines. I shook my head to clear it a bit and decided I'd better lay off the bottle for a while.

Then I realized that what he'd just said was a question and I begged his pardon.

"The clock on your mantel," he repeated, "is it correct?"

I managed to focus my eyes on it. Ten minutes to twelve, I said, "Yes, it's right. It's still early. You're not thinking of going, surely. I'm a little woozy at the moment, but——"

"How long will it take us to get there from here? I have directions how to reach it, of course, but you could probably estimate the time it will take us better than I can."

For a second I stared at him blankly, wondering what he was talking about.

Then I remembered.

We were going to a haunted house to hunt a Jabberwock—or something.

CHAPTER NINE

"First, the fish must be caught."
That is easy: a baby, I think, could have caught it.
"Next, the fish must be bought."
That is easy: a penny, I think would have bought it.

MAYBE you won't believe that I could have forgotten that, but I had. So much had happened between the time I'd left my house and the time I returned that it's a wonder, I suppose, that I still remembered my own name, and Yehudi's.

Ten minutes before twelve and we were due there, he'd said, at one o'clock.

"You have a car?" I asked him.

He nodded. "A few doors down. I got out at the wrong place to look for street numbers, but I was close enough that I didn't bother moving the car."

"Then somewhere between twenty and thirty minutes will get us there," I told him.

"Fine, Doctor. Then we've got forty minutes yet if we allow half an hour."

The woozy spell was passing fast, but I refilled his glass this time without refilling my own. I wanted to sober up a bit—not completely, because if I was sober, I might get sensible and decide not to go, and I didn't want to decide not to go.

Smith had settled back in his chair, not looking at me, so I looked at him, and wondered what I was doing even to listen to the absurd story he'd told me about Vorpal Blades and the old Wentworth house.

He wasn't the escaped lunatic, but that didn't mean he wasn't a screwball, and that I wasn't a worse one. What the hell *were* we going to do out there? Try to fish a Bandersnatch out of limbo? Or break through a looking-glass or dive down a rabbit hole to go hunting one in its native element?

Well, as long as I didn't get sober enough to spoil things, it was wonderful. Crazy or not, I was having a marvellous time. The best time I'd had since the Halloween almost forty years ago when we——But never mind that; it's a sign of old age to reminisce about the things you did when you were young, and I'm not old yet. Not very, anyway.

Yes, my eyes were focusing all right again now, but the mistiness in the room was still there and I realized that it wasn't mistiness but smoke. I looked across at the window and wondered if I wanted it open badly enough to get up and open it.

The window. A black square framing the night.

The midnight. *Where were you at midnight?* With Yehudi. *Who's Yehudi?* A little man who wasn't there. But I have the card. *Let's see it, Doc. Hmmm. What's your bug number?* My bug number?

And the black rook takes the white knight.

The smoke was definitely too thick, and so was I. I walked to the window and threw up the bottom sash. The lights behind me made it a mirror. There was my reflection. An insignificant little man with greying hair, and glasses, and a necktie badly askew.

He grinned at me and straightened his necktie. I remembered the verse from Carroll that Al Grainger had quoted at me early in the evening:

> *"You are old, Father William," the young man said.*
> *"And your hair has become very white.*
> *And yet you incessantly stand on your head.*
> *Do you think, at your age, it is right?"*

And that made me think of Al Grainger. I wondered if there was still any chance of his showing up. I'd told him to come around any time up to midnight and it was that now. I wished now that he would come. Not for chess, as we'd planned, but so he could go along on our expedition. Not that I was exactly afraid, but—well, I wished that Al Grainger would show up.

It occurred to me that he might have come or phoned and that Yehudi had failed to mention it. I asked him,

He shook his head. "No, Doc. Nobody came and the only phone call was the one you yourself made just before you came home."

So that was that, unless Al showed up in the next half hour or unless I phoned him. And I didn't want to do that. I'd been enough of a coward earlier in the evening.

Just the same I felt a little hollow——

My God, I *was* hollow. I'd had a sandwich late in the afternoon, but that had been eight hours ago and I hadn't eaten anything since. No wonder the last couple of drinks had hit me.

I suggested to Yehudi that we raid the icebox and he said it sounded like a wonderful idea to him. And it must have been, for it turned out that he was hungry as I. Between us we killed a pound of boiled ham, most of a loaf of rye and a medium-sized jar of pickles.

It was almost half-past twelve when we finished. There was just time for a stirrup cup, and we had one. With food in my stomach, it tasted much better and went down much more smoothly than the last one had. It tasted so good, in fact, that I decided to take the bottle—we'd started the second one by then—along with us. We might, after all, run into a blizzard.

"Ready to go?" Smith asked.

I decided I'd better put the window down. In its reflecting pane, over my shoulder I could see Yehudi Smith standing by the door waiting for me. The reflection was clear and sharp; it brought out the bland roundness of his face, the laughter-tracks around his mouth and eyes, the rotund absurdity of his body.

And an impulse made me walk over and hold out my hand to him and shake his hand when he put it into mine rather wonderingly. We hadn't shaken hands when we'd introduced ourselves on the porch and something made me want to do it now. I don't mean that I'm clairvoyant. I'm not, or I'd never have gone. No, I don't know why I shook hands with him.

Just an impulse, but one I'm very glad I followed. Just as I'm glad I'd given him food and drink instead of letting him go to his strange death sober or on an empty stomach.

And I'm even gladder that I said, "Smitty, I like you."

He looked pleased, but somehow embarrassed. He said, "Thanks, Doc," but for the first time his eyes didn't quite meet mine.

We went out and walked up the quiet street to where he'd left his car, and got in.

It's odd how clearly you remember some things and how vague others are. I recall that there was a push-button radio on the dashboard and that the button for WBBM was pushed in, and I recall that the gear shift knob was brightly polished onyx. But I don't recall whether the car was a coupé or a sedan, and haven't the vaguest idea what make or colour it was. I recall that the engine was quite noisy—my only clue as to whether it was an old car or a new one, that and the fact that the gear shift was on the floor and not on the steering-wheel post.

I remembered that he drove well and carefully and talked little, probably because of the noisiness of the motor.

I directed him, but I don't recall now, not that it matters, what route we took. I remember, though, that I didn't recognize the driveway of the old Wentworth place—the house itself was set quite far back from the road and you couldn't see it through the trees even in daylight—but a little farther on I recognized the farm that an aunt and uncle of mine had lived in many years ago and knew we'd passed our objective.

He turned back, then, and this time I spotted the driveway and we turned in and followed the drive back among the trees to the house itself. We parked alongside it.

"First ones here," Smith said in the hushed silence as he turned off the engine.

I got out of the car and—I don't know why; or do I?—I took the bottle with me. It was so dark outside that I couldn't see the bottle in front of my eyes as I tilted it upward.

Smith had turned out the headlights and was getting out of his side of the car. He had a flashlight in his hand and I could see again as he came around to my side of the car. I held out the bottle to him and said, "Want one?" and he said, "You read my mind, Doc," and took one. My eyes were getting a little used to the dark now and I could see the outlines of the house, and I thought about it.

God, but the place must be old, I realized. I knew it well from the weeks in summer when, as a kid, I'd visited my aunt and uncle just down the road for a taste of farm life—as against the big city of Carmel City, Illinois.

That had been over forty years ago and it had been old then, and un-tenanted. It had been lived in since, but for brief intervals. Why the few people who had tried to live there had left, I didn't know. They'd never complained—publicly, at least—of its being haunted. But none had ever stayed there for long. Perhaps it was merely the house itself; it really was a depressing place. A year or more ago the *Clarion* had carried an ad for the rental of it—and at a very reasonable price—but no one had taken it.

I thought of Johnny Haskins, who lived on the farm between my uncle's place and this one. He and I had explored the place several times together, in daylight. Johnny was dead now. He'd been killed in France in 1918, near the end of the First World War. In daytime, I hope, for Johnny had always been afraid of the dark—just as I was afraid of heights and as Al Grainger was afraid of fire and as everyone is afraid of something or other.

Johnny had been afraid of the old Wentworth place, too—even more afraid than I was, although he was several years older than I. He'd be-lieved in ghosts, a little; at least he'd been afraid of them, although not as afraid as he was of the dark. And I'd picked up a little of that fear from him and I'd kept it for quite a few years after I grew up.

But not any more. The older you get the less afraid of ghosts you are—whether you believe in them or not. By the time you pass the fifty mark you've known so many people who are now dead that ghosts, if there are any such, aren't all strangers. Some of your best friends are ghosts; why should you be afraid of them? And it's not too many years before you'll all be on the other side of the fence yourself.

No, I wasn't afraid of ghosts or the dark or of the haunted house, but I was afraid of something. I wasn't afraid of Yehudi Smith, I liked him too well to be afraid of him. Undoubtedly I was a fool to come here with him, knowing nothing at all about him. Yet I would have bet money at long odds that he wasn't dangerous. A crackpot, maybe, but not a danger-ous one.

Smith opened the car door again and said, "I just remembered I brought candles; they told me the electricity wouldn't be on. And there's another flashlight in here, if you want one, Doc."

Sure I wanted one. I felt a little better, a little less afraid of whatever I was afraid of once I had a flashlight of my own and was in no sudden danger of being alone in darkness.

I ran the beam of the flashlight up on the porch, and the house was just as I remembered it. It had been lived in just often enough for it to have been kept in repair, or at least in fairly good shape.

Yehudi Smith said, "Come on, Doc. We might as well wait inside," and led the way up the porch steps. They creaked as we walked up them but they were solid.

The front door wasn't locked. Smith must have known that it wouldn't be, from the confident way he opened it.

We went in and he closed the door behind us. The beams of our flashlights danced ahead of us down the long dimness of the hallway. I noticed with surprise that the place was carpeted and furnished; it had been empty and bare at the time I'd explored it as a kid. The most recent tenant or owner who had lived here, for whatever reason he had moved away, had left the place furnished, possibly hoping to rent or sell it that way.

We turned into a huge living-room on the left of the hallway. There was furniture there, too, white-sheeted. Covered fairly recently, from the fact that the sheets were not too dirty nor was there a great amount of dust anywhere.

Something made the back of my neck prickle. Maybe the ghostly appearance of that sheeted furniture.

"Shall we wait here or go up in the attic?" Smith asked me.

"The attic? Why the attic?"

"Where the meeting is to be held."

I was getting to like this less and less. *Was* there going to be a meeting? Were others really coming here tonight?

It was five minutes of one o'clock already.

I looked around and wondered whether I'd rather stay here or go on up into the attic. Either alternative seemed crazy. Why didn't I go home? Why hadn't I stayed there?

I didn't like that spectral white-covered furniture. I said, "Let's go on up into the attic. Might as well, I guess."

Yes, I'd come this far. I might as well see it through the rest of the way. If there was a looking-glass up there in the attic and he wanted us to walk through it, I'd do that, too. Provided only that he went first.

But I wanted another short nip out of that bottle I was carrying. I offered it to Smith and he shook his head so I went ahead and took the nip and it slightly warmed the coldness that was beginning to develop in my stomach.

We went up the stairs to the second floor and we didn't meet any ghosts or any snarks. We opened the door that led to the steps to the attic.

We walked up them, Smith in the lead and I following, his plump posterior just ahead of me.

My mind kept reminding me how ridiculous this was. How utterly insane it was for me to have come here at all.

Where were you at one o'clock? In a haunted house. *Doing what?* Waiting for the Vorpal Blades to come. *What are these Vorpal Blades?* I don't know. *What were they going to do?* I don't know, I tell you. Maybe anything. Get with child a mandrake root. Hold court to see who stole the tarts or put the white knight back on his horse. Or maybe only read the minutes of the last meeting and the treasurer's report, by Benchley. *Who's Benchley?* WHO'S YEHUDI?

Who's your little whoozis?

Doc, I hate to say this, but——

I'm afraid that——

Very pitying, and oh, so sensibly true. *You were drunk, weren't you, Doc?* Well, not exactly, but——

Yehudi Smith's plump posterior ascending the attic stairs. A horse's posterior ascending after him.

We reached the top and Smith asked me to hold my flashlight aimed at the post of the stair railing until he got a candle lighted there. He took a short, thick candle from his pocket—one that would balance easily by itself without a holder—and got it lighted.

There were trunks and a few pieces of broken or worn out furniture scattered about the sides of the attic; the middle of it was clear. The only window was at the back and it was boarded up from the inside.

I looked around and, although the furniture here wasn't sheeted, I didn't like the place any better than I'd liked the big room downstairs. The light of one candle was far too dim to dispel the darkness, for one thing, in so large a space. And I didn't like the flickering shadows it cast. They might have been Jabberwocks or anything your imagination wanted to name them. There ought to be Rorschach tests with flickering shadows; what the mind would make out of them ought to be a lot more revealing than what the mind makes out of ink blots.

Yes, I could have used more light, a lot more light. But Smith had put his flashlight in his pocket and I did the same with the other one; it was his, too, and I didn't have any excuse to wear out the battery keeping it on. And besides it didn't do much good in so large a room.

"What do we do now?" I asked.

"Wait for the others. What time is it, Doc?"

I managed to read my watch by the light of the candle and told him that it was seven minutes after one.

He nodded. "We'll give them until a quarter after. There's something that I must do then, at the exact time, whether they're here or not. Listen, isn't that a car?"

I listened and I thought it was. Way up here in the attic, it wasn't clearly audible, but I thought I heard a car that could have been coming back from the main road to the house. I was pretty sure of it.

I uncorked the bottle again and offered it. This time Smith took a drink, too. Mine was a fairly long pull. I was getting sober, I thought, and this was no time or place to get sober. It was silly enough to be here, drunk.

I couldn't hear the car any more, and then suddenly—as though it had stopped and then started again—I could hear it, and louder than before. But the sound seemed to diminish as though the car had driven back from the road, stopped a minute, and then headed for the main road again. The sound died out.

The shadows flickered. There was no sound from downstairs.

I shivered a little.

Smith said, "Help me look for something, Doc. It's supposed to be here somewhere, ready. A small table."

"A table?"

"Yes, but don't touch if it you find it."

He had his flashlight out again and was working his way along one wall of the attic, and I went the other way, glad of a chance to use my flashlight on those damned shadows. I wondered what the hell kind of a table I was looking for. Thou prepares a table before me in the presence of mine enemies, I thought. But there weren't any of my enemies here, I hoped.

I found it first. It was in the back corner of the attic.

It was a small, three-legged, glass-topped table, and there were two small objects lying on it.

I started laughing. Ghosts and shadows or not, I laughed out loud. One of the objects on the table was a small key and the other was a small vial with a tag tied to it.

The glass-topped table Alice had found in the hall at the bottom of the rabbit hole—the table on which had been the key that opened the little door to the garden and the bottle with the paper label that said, "DRINK ME" tied around its neck.

I'd seen that table often—in the John Tenniel illustration of it in *Alice in Wonderland*.

Smith's footsteps coming up behind me made me stop laughing. After all, this ridiculous flummery might be something of a ritual to him. It was funny to me, but I liked him and I didn't want to hurt his feelings.

He wasn't even smiling. He said. "Yes, that's it. Is it one-fifteen yet?"

"Almost on the head."

"Good." He picked up the key with one hand and the bottle with the other. "The others must be delayed, but we shall take the first step. This, keep." He dropped the key into my pocket. "And this, I drink." He took the cork out of the bottle. "I apologize for not being able to share it with you—as you have so generously shared your drinks with me—but you understand, until you have been fully initiated——"

He seemed genuinely embarrassed, so I nodded understanding and forgiveness.

I wasn't afraid any more, now. It had become too ridiculous for fear. What was that "drink me" bottle supposed to do? Oh, yes, he'd shrink in size until he was only a few inches high—and then he'd have to find and use a little box labelled "EAT ME" and eat the cake inside and he'd suddenly grow so big that——

He lifted the bottle and said, "To Lewis Carroll."

Since that was the toast, I said, "Wait!" and got the cork quickly out of the bottle of whisky I was still carrying, and raised it, too. There wasn't any reason why I couldn't and shouldn't get in on that toast as long as my lips, as a neophyte's, didn't defile whatever sacred elixir the "drink me" bottle held.

He clinked the little bottle lightly against the big one I held, and tossed it off—I could see from the corner of my eye as I tilted my bottle—in that strange conjuring trick again, the bottle stopping inches away from his lips and the drink keeping on going without the loss of a drop.

I was putting the cork into the whisky bottle when Yehudi Smith died.

He dropped the bottle labelled "DRINK ME" and started to clutch at his throat, but he died, I think, even before the bottle hit the floor. His face was hideously contorted with pain, but the pain couldn't have lasted over a fraction of a second. His eyes, still open, went suddenly blank, utterly blank. And the thud of his fall shook the floor under my feet, seemed to shake the whole house.

CHAPTER TEN

And as in uffish thought he stood,
The Jabberwock, with eyes of flame,
Came whiffling through the tulgey wood,
And burbled as it came!

I THINK I must have done nothing but stand there and jitter for seconds. Finally I was able to move.

I'd seen his face and I'd seen and heard him fall; I didn't have the slightest doubt that he was dead. But I had to be sure. I got down on my knees and groped my hand inside his coat and shirt, hunting for a heartbeat. There wasn't any.

I made even surer. The flashlight he'd given me had a round flat lens; I held it over his mouth and in front of his nostrils for a while and there was no slightest trace of moisture.

The small empty bottle from which he'd drunk was of fairly heavy glass. It hadn't broken when he'd dropped it, and the tag tied around its neck had kept it from rolling far. I didn't touch it, but I got on my hands and knees and sniffed at the open end. The smell was the smell of good whisky, nothing else that I could detect. No odour of bitter almonds, but if what had been in that whisky hadn't been prussic acid it had been some corrosive poison just about as strong. Or could it have been prussic, and would the smell of whisky have blanketed the bitter almond smell? I didn't know.

I stood up again and found that my knees were shaking. This was the second man I'd seen die tonight. But I hadn't so much minded about George. He'd had it coming, for one thing, and for another his body had been inside the crumpled-up car; I'd not actually seen him die. Nor had I been alone then; Smiley had been with me. I'd have given my whole bank account, all three hundred and twelve dollars of it, to have had Smiley with me there in the attic.

I wanted to get out of there, fast, and I was too scared to move. I thought I'd be less scared if I could figure out what it was all about, but it was sheerly mad. It didn't make sense that even a madman would have brought me out here under so weird a pretext so that I could be an audience of one to his suicide.

In fact, if I was sure of anything, I was sure that Smith hadn't killed himself. But who had, and why? The Vorpal Blades? *Was* there such a group?

Where were they? Why hadn't they come?

A sudden thought put shivers down my spine. *Maybe they had.* I'd thought I heard a car come and go, while we'd waited. Why couldn't it have dropped off passengers? Waiting for me downstairs—or even now creeping up the attic steps towards me.

I looked that way. The candle flickered and the shadows danced. I strained my ears, but there wasn't any sound. No sound anywhere.

I was afraid to move, and then gradually I found that I was afraid not to move. I had to get *out* of here before I went crazy. If anything was downstairs I'd rather go down and meet it than wait till it decided to come up here after me.

I wished to hell and back that I hadn't given Smiley that revolver, but wishing didn't get me the revolver back.

Well, the whisky bottle was a weapon of sorts. I shifted the flashlight to my left hand and picked up the whisky bottle, by its neck, in my right. It was still more than half-full and heavy enough for a bludgeon.

I tiptoed to the head of the steps. I don't know why I tiptoed unless it was to avoid scaring myself worse by making noise; we hadn't been quiet up here before and Smith's fall had shaken the whole house. If anyone was downstairs, he knew he wasn't alone in the building.

I looked at the square post at the top of the railing and the short, thick candle still burning on top of it. I didn't want to touch it; I wanted to be able to say that I hadn't touched anything at all, except to feel for a heartbeat that wasn't there. Yet I couldn't leave the candle burning, either; it might set the house afire if it fell over, as Smith hadn't anchored it down with molten wax but had merely stood it on its base.

I compromised by blowing it out but not touching it otherwise.

My flashlight showed me there was nothing or no one on the stairs leading down to the second floor and that the door at the bottom of them was still closed, as we had left it. Before I started down them I took one last look around the attic with my flash. The shadows jumped as the beam swept around the walls, and then, for some reason, I brought the circle of light to rest on Yehudi Smith's body lying sprawled there on the floor, eyes wide open and still staring unseeingly at the rafters overhead, his face still frozen in the grimace of that horrible, if brief, pain in which he'd died.

I hated to leave him alone there in the dark. Silly and sentimental as the thought was. I couldn't help feeling that way. He'd been such a nice little guy. Who the hell had killed him, and why, and why in such a bizarre manner, and what was it all about? And he'd said it was dangerous to come here tonight, and he was dead right, as far as he himself was concerned. And I——?

With that thought, I was afraid again. I wasn't out of here yet. Was someone or something waiting downstairs?

The attic stairs were uncarpeted and they squeaked so loudly that I gave up trying to walk quietly and hurried. The attic door creaked, too, but nothing was waiting for me on the other side of it. Or downstairs, I flashed my light into the big living room as I passed the doorway and got a momentary fright as I thought something white was coming toward me—but it was only the sheeted table and it had only seemed to move.

The porch and down the porch steps.

The car was still there on the driveway beside the house. It was a coupé, I noticed now, and the same make and model as mine. My feet crunched gravel as I walked to it; I was still scared but I didn't dare let myself run. I wondered if Smith had left the key in the car, and hoped frantically that he had. I should have thought of it while I was still in the attic and could have felt in his pockets. I wouldn't go back up there now, I realized, for anything in the world. I'd walk back to town first.

At least the car door wasn't locked. I slid in under the wheel, and flashed my light on the dashboard. Yes, the ignition key was in the lock. I slammed the door behind me and felt a little more secure inside the closed car.

I turned the key and stepped on the starter and the engine started the first try. I shifted into low gear and then, before I let out the clutch, I carefully shifted back into neutral again and sat there with the motor idling.

This wasn't the car in which Yehudi Smith had driven me here. The gear shift knob was hard rubber with a ridge around it, not the smooth onyx ball I'd noticed on the gear shift lever of his car. It was like the one on my car, which was back home in the garage with two flat tyres that I hadn't got around to fixing.

I turned on the dome light, although by then I didn't really have to. I knew already from the feel of the controls in starting and in shifting, from the sound of the engine, from a dozen little things.

This was *my car.*

It was so impossible that I forgot to be afraid, that I was in such a hurry to get away from the house. Oh, there was a little logic in my lack of fear, too; if anybody had been laying for me, the house would have been the place. He wouldn't have let me get this far and he wouldn't have left the ignition key in the car so I could get away in it.

I got out of the car and looked, with the flashlight, at the two tyres which had been flat this morning. They weren't flat now. Either someone had fixed them, or someone had simply let the air out of them last night and had subsequently pumped them up again with the hand pump I keep in my luggage compartment. The second idea seemed more likely; now that I thought of it, it was strange that two tyres—both in good shape and with good tubes in them—should have gone flat, completely flat, at the same time and while the car was standing in my garage.

I walked all the way around the car, looking at it, and there wasn't anything wrong with it that I could see. I got back in under the wheel and sat there a minute with the engine running, wondering if it was even remotely possible that Yehudi Smith had driven me here in my own car.

No, I decided, not remotely. I hadn't noticed his car at all except for three things, but those three things were plenty to make me sure. Beside the gear shift knob, I remembered that push-button radio with the button for WBBM pushed in—and my car has no radio at all—and there was the fact that his engine was noisy and mine is quiet. Right then, with it idling, I could barely hear it.

Unless I was crazy——

Could I have imagined that other car? For that matter, could I have imagined Yehudi Smith? Could I have driven out here by myself in my own car, gone up to the attic alone——?

It's a horrible thing to suspect yourself suddenly of complete insanity, equipped with hallucinations.

I realized I'd better quit thinking along those lines, here alone in a car, alone in the night, parked beside a haunted house. I might drive myself nutty, if I wasn't already.

I took a long drink out of the bottle that was now on the seat beside me, and then drove out to the highway and back to town. I didn't drive fast, partly because I was a little drunk—physically anyway. The horrible thing that had happened up in the attic, the fantastic, incredible death of Yehudi Smith, had shocked me sober, mentally.

I *couldn't* have imagined——

But at the edge of town the doubts came back, then the answer to them. I pulled to the side of the road and turned on the dome light. I had the card and the key and the flashlight, those three souvenirs of my experience. I took the flashlight out of my coat pocket and looked at it. Just a dime-store flashlight; it meant nothing except that it wasn't mine. The card was the thing. I hunted in several pockets, getting worried as hell, before I found it in the pocket of my shirt. Yes, I had it, and it still read *Yehudi Smith*. I felt a little better as I put it back in my pocket. While I was at it, I looked at the key, too. The key that had been with the "Drink Me" bottle on the glass-topped table.

It was still there in the pocket Smith had dropped it into; I'd not touched it or looked at it closely. It was, of course, the wrong kind of key, but I'd noticed that at first glance when I'd seen it on the table in the attic; that had been part of my source of amusement when I'd laughed. It was a Yale key, and it should have been a small gold key, the one Alice used to open the fifteen-inch-high door into the lovely garden.

Come to think of it, all three of those props in the attic had been wrong, one way or another. The table had been a glass-topped one, but it should have been an all-glass table; the wooden legs were wrong. The key shouldn't have been a nickel-plated Yale, and the "Drink Me" should not have contained poison. (*It had, in fact, a sort of mixed flavour of cherry-tart, custard, pine-apple, roast turkey, toffy, and hot buttered toast* – according to Alice.) It couldn't have tasted anything like that to Smith.

I started driving again, slowly. Now that I was back in town I had to make up my mind whether I was going to the sheriffs office or going to call the state police. Reluctantly I decided I'd better go right to the sheriff. Definitely this case was in his department, unless he called on the state police for help. They'd dump it in his lap anyway, even if I called them. And he hated my guts enough as it was, without my making it any worse by by-passing him in reporting a major crime. Not that I didn't hate his guts just as much, but tonight he was in a better position to make trouble for me than I was for him.

So I parked my coupé across the street from the courthouse and took one more swig from the bottle to give me courage to tell Kates the story I was going to have to tell him. Then I marched myself across the street and up the courthouse stairs to the sheriffs office on the second floor. If I was lucky, I thought, Kates might be out and his deputy, Hank Ganzer, might be there.

I wasn't lucky. Hank wasn't there at all, and Kates was talking on the phone. He glared at me when I came in and then went back to his call.

"Hell, I could have done it on the phone from here. Go see the guy. Wake him up and be sure he's awake enough to remember any little thing that might have been said. Yeah, then call me again before you start back."

He put the receiver down and his swivel chair squeaked shrilly as he swung about to face me. He yelled, "There isn't any story on it yet." Rance Kates always yells; I've never heard him say anything in a quiet tone, or even a normal one. His voice matches his red face, which always looks angry. I've often wondered if he looks like that even when he's in bed. Wondered, but had no inclination to find out.

What he'd just yelled at me, though, made so little sense that I just looked at him.

I said, "I've come to report a murder, Kates."

"Huh?" He looked interested. "You mean you found either Miles or Bonney?"

For a minute neither name registered at all. I said, "The man's name is Smith." I thought I'd better sneak up on the Yehudi part gradually, maybe let Kates read it himself off the card. "The body is in the attic of the old Wentworth place out on the pike."

"Stoeger, are you drunk?"

"I've been drinking," I told him. "I'm not drunk." At least I hoped I wasn't. Maybe that last one I'd taken in the car just before I'd left it had been one too many. My voice sounded thick, even to me, and I had a hunch my eyes were looking a trifle bleary from the outside; they were beginning to feel that way from my side of them.

"What were you doing in the attic of the Wentworth place? You mean you were there tonight?"

I wished again that Hank Ganzer had been there instead of Kates. Hank would have taken my word for it and gone out for the body; then my story wouldn't have sounded so incredible when I'd have got around to telling it.

I said, "Yes, I just came from there. I went there with Smith; at his request."

"Who is this Smith? You know him?"

"I met him tonight for the first time. He came to see me."

"What for? What were you doing out there? A haunted house!"

I sighed. There wasn't anything I could do but answer his damn questions and they were getting tougher all the time. Let's see, how could I put it so it wouldn't sound *too* crazy?

I said, "We went there because it *is* supposed to be a haunted house, Kates. This Smith was interested in the occult—in psychic phenomena. He asked me to go out there with him to perform an experiment. I gathered that some other people were coming, but they didn't."

"What kind of an experiment?"

"I don't know. He was killed before we got around to it."

"You and him were there alone?"

"Yes," I said, but I saw where that was leading so I added, "But I didn't kill him. And I don't know who did. He was poisoned."

"Poisoned how?"

Part of my brain wanted to tell him, "Out of a little bottle labelled 'DRINK ME' on a glass table, as in *Alice in Wonderland.*" The sensible part of my brain told me to let him find that out for himself. I said, "Out of a bottle that was planted there for him to drink. By whom, I don't know.

But you sound like you don't believe me. Why don't you go out and see for yourself, Kates? Damn it, man, I'm reporting a *murder*." And then it occurred to me there wasn't really any proof of that, so I amended it a little: "Or at least a death of violence."

He stared at me and I think he was becoming convinced, a little.

His phone rang and his swivel chair screamed again as he swung around. He barked "Hello. Sheriff Kates," into it.

Then his voice tamed down a little. He said, "No, Mrs. Harrison, haven't heard a thing. Hank's over at Neilsville, checking up at that end, and he's going to watch the road again on his way back. I'll call you the minute I learn anything at all. But don't worry; it can't be anything serious."

He turned back. "Stoeger, if this is a *gag*, I'm going to take you apart." He meant it, and he could do it, too. Kates is only a medium-sized man, not too much bigger than I, but he's tough and hard as a rock physically. He can handle men weighing half again as much as he does. And he's got enough of a sadistic streak to enjoy doing it whenever he has a good excuse for it.

"It's no gag," I said. "What's this about Miles Harrison and Ralph Bonney?"

"Missing. They left Neilsville with the Bonney pay roll a little after half past eleven and should have been back here around midnight. It's almost two o'clock and nobody knows where they are. Look, if I thought you were sober and there *was* a stiff out on the pike, I'd call the state cops. I *got* to stay here till we find what happened to Miles and Bonney."

The state cops were fine, as far as I was concerned. I'd reported it where it should have been reported, and Kates would have no kickback if he himself called the state police. I was just opening my mouth to say that might be a good idea when the phone rang again.

Kates yelled into it, and then, "As far as the teller knew, they were heading right back, Hank? Nothing unusual happened at that end, huh? Okay, come back; and watch both sides of the road all the way in case they ran off it or something. . . . Yeah, the pike. That's the only way they could've come. Oh, and listen, stop at the Wentworth place on your way and take a look in the attic . . . Yeah, I said the attic. Doc Stoeger's here, drunk as a coot, and he says there's a stiff in the attic there. If there *is* one, I'll worry about it."

He slammed the receiver down and started shuffling papers on his desk, trying to look busy. Finally he thought of something to do and phoned the Bonney Fireworks Company to see if Bonney had showed up there yet, or called them. Apparently, from what I could hear of the conversation, he hadn't done either.

I realized that I was still standing up and that now, since Kates had given that order to his deputy, nothing was going to happen until Hank got back—at least half an hour if he drove slowly to watch both sides of the road. So I found myself a chair and sat down. Kates shuffled papers again and paid no attention to me.

I got to wondering about Bonney and Miles, and hoped they hadn't had an accident. If they had had one, and were two hours overdue, it must have been a bad one. Unless both were seriously hurt, one of them would have reached a phone long before this. Of course they could have stopped somewhere for a drink, but it didn't seem likely, not for two hours at least. And, come to think of it, they couldn't have; the closing hour for taverns applied to the whole county, not just to Carmel City. Twelve o'clock had been almost two hours ago.

I wished that it wasn't. Not that I either needed or wanted a drink particularly at that moment, but it would have been much more pleasant to do my waiting at Smiley's instead of here in the sheriff's office.

Kates suddenly swivelled his chair at me, "*You* don't know anything about Bonney and Harrison, do you?"

"Not a thing," I told him.

"Where were you at midnight?"

With Yehudi. Who's Yehudi? *The little man who wasn't there.*

I said, "Home, talking to Smith. We stayed there until half past twelve."

"Anybody else there?"

I shook my head. Come to think of it, nobody but myself had, as far as I knew, even seen Yehudi Smith. If his body *wasn't* in the attic at the Wentworth place, I was going to have a hell of a time proving he'd ever existed. A card and a key and a flashlight.

"Where's this Smith guy come from?"

"I don't know. He didn't say."

"What was his first name?"

I stalled on that one. I said, "I don't remember. I've got his card some-where. He gave me one." Let him think the card was probably out at the house. I wasn't ready to show it to him yet.

"How'd he happen to come to *you* to go to a haunted house with him if he didn't even know you?"

I said, "He knew *of* me, as a Lewis Carroll fan."

"A what?"

"Lewis Carroll. *Alice in Wonderland, Alice Through the Looking-Glass.*" And a "DRINK ME" bottle on a glass table, and a key, and Bandersnatches and Jabberwocks. But let Kates find that out for himself, after he'd found a body and knew that I wasn't either drunk or crazy.

He said, *"Alice in Wonderland!"* and sniffed. He glared at me a full ten seconds and then decided, apparently, that he was wasting his time on me and swivelled back to his paper shuffling.

I felt in my pockets to make sure that the card and the key were still there. They were. The flashlight was still in the car, but the flashlight didn't mean anything anyway. Maybe the key didn't either. But the card was my contact with reality, in a sense. As long as it still said *Yehudi Smith*, I knew I wasn't stark raving mad. I knew that there'd really been such a person and that he wasn't a figment of my imagination.

I slipped it out of my pocket to look at it again. Yes, it still said, *"Yehudi Smith"*, although my eyes had a bit of trouble focusing on it clearly. The printing looked fuzzy, which meant I needed either one more drink or several less.

Yehudi Smith, in fuzzy-edged type. Yehudi, the little man who wasn't there.

And suddenly—don't ask me how I knew, but I knew. I didn't see the pattern, but I saw that much of it. The little man who wasn't there.

Wouldn't be there.

Hank was going to come in and say, "What's this about a stiff in the Wentworth attic? *I* couldn't find one."

Yehudi. The little man who wasn't there. *I saw a man upon the stair, A little man who wasn't there. He wasn't there again today; Gee, I wish he'd go away.*

It was preordained; it *had* to be. That much of the pattern I saw. The name Yehudi hadn't been an accident. I think that *almost*, just then, I had a flash of insight that would have shown me most of the pattern, if not all of it. You know how it is sometimes when you're drunk, but not too drunk, you think you're trembling on the verge of understanding something important and cosmic that has eluded you all your life? And—just barely possibly—you really are. I think I was, at that moment.

Then I looked up from the card and the thread of my thought was lost because Kates was staring at me. He'd turned just his head this time instead of the squeaking swivel chair he was sitting on. He was looking at me speculatively, suspiciously.

I tried to ignore it; I was trying to recapture my thoughts and let them lead me. I was close to something. *I saw a man upon the stair.* Yehudi Smith's plump posterior ascending the attic stairs, just ahead of me.

No, the dead body with the contorted face—the poor piece of cold clay that had been a nice little guy with laughter lines around his eyes and the corners of his mouth—wouldn't be there in the attic when Hank Ganzer looked for it. It couldn't be there; its presence there wouldn't fit the pattern that I still couldn't see or understand.

Squeal of the swivel chair as Rance Kates turned his body to match the position of his head. "Is that the card that guy gave you?"

I nodded.

"What's his full name?"

The hell with Kates. "Yehudi," I said. "Yehudi Smith."

Of course it wasn't really; I knew at least that much now. I got up and walked to Kates' desk. Unfortunately for my dignity, I weaved a little. But I made it without falling. I put the card down in front of him and went back and sat down again, managing to walk straight this time.

He looked at the card and then at me and then at the card and then at me.

And then I knew I *must* be crazy.

"Doc,' he asked—and his voice was quieter than I'd ever heard it before – "*what's your bug number?*"

CHAPTER ELEVEN

"O Oysters," said the Carpenter,
"You've had a pleasant run!
Shall we be trotting home again?"
But answer came there none——

I JUST stared at him. Either he was crazy or I was——and several times in the last hour I'd been wondering about myself. *What's your bug number?* What a question to ask a man in the spot I was in. What's yours?

Finally I managed to answer. "Huh?" I said.

"Your bug number. Your label number."

I got it then. I wasn't crazy after all. I knew what he meant.

I run a union shop, which means that I've signed a contract with the International Typographical Union and pay Pete, my only employee, union wages. In a town as small as Carmel City, you can get by with a non-union shop, but I happen to believe in unions and to think the Typographical Union is a good one. Being a union shop, we put the union label on everything we print. It's a little oval-shaped dingus, so small you can barely read the type if you've got good eyesight. And alongside it is an equally tiny number which is the number of my particular shop among the other union shops in my area. By the combination of the place name which is part of the label itself and the number of the shop beside it, you can tell where any given piece of union printing has been done.

But that little oval logotype is known to non-union printers as "the bug". It does, I'll admit, look rather like a tiny bug crawling across the bottom corner of whatever it's put on. And non-union printers call the shop number alongside the "bug" the "bug number." Kates wasn't a printer, union or otherwise, but I remember now that two of his brothers, both living in Neilsville, were non-union printers, and naturally he'd have picked up the language—and the implied prejudice back of it—from them.

I said, "My label number is seven."

He slapped the calling card down on the desk in front of him. He snorted—quite literally; you often read about people snorting but seldom hear them do it. He said, "Stoeger, you printed this damn thing yourself. The whole thing is a gag. Damn you——"

He started to get up and then sat down again and looked at the papers in front of him. He looked back at me and I think he was going to tell me to get the hell out, and then apparently he decided he might as well wait till Hank got back.

He shuffled papers.

I sat there and tried to absorb the fact that—apparently, at any rate—that *Yehudi Smith* calling card had been printed in my own shop. I didn't get up to look at it. Somehow, I was perfectly willing to take Kates' word for it.

Why not? It was part of the pattern. I should have guessed it myself. Not from the typeface; almost every shop has eight-point Garamond. But from the fact that the "DRINK ME" bottle had contained poison and Yehudi wasn't going to be there when Hank looked for him. It followed the pattern, and I knew now what the pattern was. It was the pattern of madness.

Mine—or whose? I was getting scared. I'd been scared several times already that night, but this was a different variety of scared-ness. I was getting scared of the night itself, of the *pattern* of the night.

I needed a drink, and I needed it bad. I stood up and started for the door. The swivel chair screamed and Kates said, "Where the hell you think you're going?"

"Down to my car. Going to get something. I'll be back." I didn't want to get into an argument with him.

"Sit down. You're not going out of here."

I did want to get into an argument with him. "Am I under arrest? And on what charge?"

"Material witness in a murder case, Stoeger. *If* there's a corpse where you say there's one. If there isn't, we can switch it to drunk and disorderly. Take your choice.

I took my choice. I sat down again.

He had me over a barrel and I could see that he loved it. I wished that I'd gone to my office and phoned the state police, regardless of repercussions.

I waited. That "bug number" angle of Kates' had thrown me off thinking about how it could be and why it would be that Yehudi Smith's calling card had been printed in my own print shop. Not that, come to think of it, the "how" had been difficult. I lock the door when I leave, but I lock it with a dime-store skeleton key. They come two on a card for a dime. Yes, Anybody could have got in. And Anybody whoever he was could have printed that card without knowing a damn thing about printing. You have to know the printer's case to set type in quantity, but anybody could pick out a dozen letters, more or less, to spell out Yehudi Smith simply by trial and error. The little hand press I print cards on is so simple that a child—well, anyway, a high school kid—could figure out how to operate it. True, he'd get lousy impressions and waste a lot of cards trying to get one good one. But Anybody, if he'd tried long enough, could have printed one good card that said *Yehudi Smith* and carried my union label in the bottom corner.

But why would Anybody have done something like that?

The more I thought about it the less sense it made, although one thing did emerge that made even less sense that the rest of it. It would have been easier to print that card without the union label than with it, so Anybody had gone to a little additional trouble to bring out the fact that the card *had* been printed at the *Clarion*. Except for the death of Yehudi Smith the whole thing might have been the pattern of a monstrous practical joke. But practical jokes don't include sudden death. Not even such a fantastic death as Yehudi Smith had met.

Why had Yehudi Smith died?

Somewhere there had to be a key.

And that reminded me of the key in my pocket and I took it out and stared at it, wondering what I could open with it. Somewhere there was a lock that it fitted.

It didn't look either familiar or unfamiliar. Yale keys don't. Could it be mine? I thought about all the keys I owned. The key to the front door of my house was a Yale type key, but not actually a Yale. Besides——

I took the keytainer from my pocket and opened it. My front door key is on the left and I compared it with the key I'd brought away from the attic. The notches didn't match; it wasn't a duplicate of that one. And it was still more different from my back door key, the one on the other side of the row. In between were two other keys but both were quite different types. One was the key to the door at the *Clarion* office and the other was for the garage behind my house. I never use the garage key; I keep nothing of value in the garage except the car itself and I always leave it locked.

It seemed to me that I'd had five keys instead of four, there on the keytainer, but I couldn't remember for sure and I couldn't figure out what the missing one was, if one really was missing.

Not the key to my car; I didn't keep that on the keytainer (I hate a keytainer dangling and swinging from my ignition lock, so I carry the car key loose in my vest pocket).

I put the keytainer back in my pocket and stared at the single key again. I wondered suddenly if it could be a duplicate of my car key. But I couldn't compare it to see because, this time, I'd left the key in the lock when I'd got out of the car, thinking I was going to be up here in the sheriff's office only a minute or two and that then he'd be heading out to the Wentworth place with me.

Kates must have turned his head—not his swivel chair, for it didn't squeak—and seen me staring at the key. He asked, "What's that?"

"A key," I said. "A key to unlock a riddle. A key to murder."

The chair did squeak then. "Stoeger, what the hell? Are you just drunk, or are you crazy?"

"I don't know," I said. "Which do you think?"

He snorted. "Let's see that key." I handed it to him.

"What's it open?"

"I don't know." I was getting mad again—not particularly at Kates this time; at everything. "I know what it's supposed to open."

"What?"

"A little door fifteen inches high off a room at the bottom of a rabbit hole. It leads to a beautiful garden."

He looked at me a long time. I looked back. I didn't give a damn.

I heard a car outside. That would be Hank Ganzer, probably. He wouldn't have found the body of Yehudi Smith in the attic out on the pike. I knew that, somehow.

And how Kates was going to react to that, I could guess. Even though, obviously, he didn't believe a damn word of it to begin with. I'd have given a lot, just then, to see inside Rance Kates' mind, or what he uses for one, to see just what he *was* thinking. I'd have given a lot more, though, to be inside the mind of Anybody, the person who'd printed Yehudi Smith's card on my hand press and who'd put the poison in the "Drink Me" bottle.

Hank's steps coming up the stairs.

He came in the door and his eyes happened to be looking in my direction first. He said, "Hi, Doc," casually and then turned to Kates. "No sign of an accident, Rance. I drove slow, watched both sides of the road. No sign of a car going off. But look, maybe we should both do it. If one of us could keep moving the spotlight back and forth while the other drove, we could see back farther." He looked at his wrist watch. "It's only two-thirty. Won't get light until six, and in that long a time——"

Kates nodded. "Okay, Hank. But listen, I'm going to get the state boys in on this case—well, in case Bonney's car turns up somewhere else. We know when they left Neilsville, but we can't be positive they started for Carmel City."

"Why wouldn't they?"

"How would I know?" Kates said. "But if they did start here, they didn't get here."

I might as well not have been there at all.

I cut in. "Hank, did you go to the Wentworth place?"

He looked at me. "Sure, Doc. Listen, what kind of a gag was that?"

"Did you look in the attic?"

"Sure. Looked all around it with my flashlight."

I'd known it, but I closed my eyes.

Kates surprised me, after all. His voice was almost gentle. "Stoeger, get the hell out of here. Go home and sleep it off."

I opened my eyes again and looked at Hank. "All right," I said, "I'm drunk or crazy. But listen, Hank, was there a candle stub standing on top of the post at the top of the attic steps?"

He shook his head slowly.

"A glass-topped table, standing in one corner—it'd be the north-west corner of the attic?"

"I didn't see it, Doc. I wasn't looking for tables. But I'd have noticed a candle stub, if it had been on the stair post. I remember putting my hand on it when I started down."

"And you don't recall seeing a dead body on the floor?"

Hank didn't even answer me. He looked back at Kates. "Rance, maybe I'd better drive Doc home while you're making those calls. Where's your car, Doc?"

"Across the street."

"Okay, we won't give you a parking ticket. I'll drive you home in mine." He looked at Kates for corroboration.

Kates gave it. I hated Kates for it. He was grinning at me. He had me in such a nasty spot that, damn him, he could afford to be generous. If he threw me in the can overnight, I could fight back. If he sent me home to sleep it off—and even gave me a chauffeur to take me there——

Hank Ganzer said, "Come on, Doc." He was going through the door.

I got to my feet. I didn't *want* to go home. If I went home now, the murderer of Yehudi Smith would have the rest of the night to finish—to finish what? And what was it to me, except that I'd liked Yehudi Smith? And who the hell was Yehudi Smith?

I said, "Listen, Kates——"

Kates looked past me at the doorway. He said, "Go on, Hank. See if his car is parked straight and then I'll send him down. I think he can make it."

He probably hoped I'd break my neck going down the steps.

"Sure, Rance." Hank's footsteps going down the stairs. Diminuendo.

Kates looked up at me. I was standing in front of his desk, trying not to look like a boy caught cheating in an examination standing in front of his teacher's desk.

I caught his eyes, and almost took a step backward. I hated Kates and knew that he hated me, but I hated him as one hates a man in office whom one knows to be a stupid oaf and a crook. He hated me, I thought, as someone who, as an editor, had power—and used it—against men like him.

But the look in his eyes wasn't that. It was *sheer personal* hatred and malevolence. It was something I hadn't suspected, and it shocked me. I don't, after fifty-three years, shock easily.

And then that look was gone, as suddenly as when you turn out a light. He was looking at me impersonally. His voice was impersonal, almost flat, not nearly as loud as usual. He said, "Stoeger, you know what I could do to you on something like this, don't you?"

I didn't answer; he didn't expect me to. Yes, I knew some of the things. The can overnight on a drunk and disorderly charge was a starting point. And if, in the morning, I persisted in my illusions, he could call in Dr. Buchan for a psychiatric once-over.

He said, "I'm not doing it. But I want you out of my hair from now on. Understand?"

I didn't answer that, either. If he wanted to think silence was consent, all right. Apparently he did. He said, "Now get the hell out of here."

I got the hell out of there. I'd got off easy. Except for that look he'd given me.

No, I didn't feel like a conquering hero about it. I should have faced up to it, and I should have insisted that there *had* been a murder in that attic, whether there was a *corpus delicti* there now or not. But I was too mixed up myself. I wanted time to think things out, to figure what the hell had really happened.

I went down the stairs and out into the night again.

Hank Ganzer's car was parked right in front, but he was just getting out of my car, across the street. I walked over toward him.

He said, "You *were* a little far out from the kerb, Doc. I moved it in for you. Here's your key."

He handed me the key and I stuck it in my pocket and then reopened the door he'd just closed to get the bottle of whisky that was lying on the seat. No use leaving that, even if I had to leave the car here.

I stepped back, then, to the back of the car to take another look at those back tyres. I still couldn't believe them; this morning they'd been completely flat. That was part of the puzzle, too.

Hank came back and stood by me. "What's the matter, Doc?" he asked. "If you're looking at your tyres, they're okay." He kicked the one nearest him and then walked around and kicked the other. He started back, and stopped.

He said, "Say, Doc, something you got in your luggage compartment must've spilled over. Did you have a can of paint or something in there?"

I shook my head and came around to see what he was looking at. It did look as though something had run out from under the bottom edge of the luggage compartment door. Something thick and blackish.

Hank turned the handle and tried to lift.

"It's not locked," I said. "I never bother to lock it. Nothing in there but a worn-out tyre without a tube in it."

He tried again. "The hell it's not locked. Where's the key?"

Another piece of the pattern fell into place. I knew now what the fifth key, the middle one, on my keytainer should have been. I never lock the luggage compartment of my car except on the rare occasions when I take a trip and really have luggage in it. But I carry the key on my keytainer. And it was a Yale key and it hadn't been there when I'd looked a few minutes ago.

I said, "Kates has got it." It had to be. One Yale key looks like another, but the card, Yehudi Smith's card, had been printed in my own shop. The key would be mine, too.

Hank said, "Huh?"

I said again, "Kates has got it."

Hank looked at me strangely. He said. "Wait just a minute, Doc," and walked across to his own car. Twice, on the way, he looked back as though to be sure I wasn't going to get in and drive away.

He got a flashlight out of his glove compartment and came back. He bent down with it and took a close look at those streaks.

I stepped closer to look, too. Hank stepped back, as though he was suddenly afraid to have me behind him and peering over his shoulder.

So I didn't have to look. I knew what those streaks were, or what Hank thought they were.

He said, "Seriously, Doc, where's the key?"

"I'm serious," I told him. "I gave it to Rance Kates. I didn't know what key it was then. I'm pretty sure I do now.

I thought I knew what was in that luggage compartment now, too.

He looked at me uncertainly and then walked part way across the street, angling so he could watch me. He cupped his hands around his lips and called out. "Rance! Hey, Rance!" And then looked quickly back to see that I was neither sneaking up on him nor trying to get into the car to drive away.

Nothing happened and he did it again.

A window opened and Kates was silhouetted against the light back of it. He called back, "What the hell, Hank, if you want me come up here. Don't wake up the whole God damn town."

Hank looked back over his shoulder at me again. Then he called, "Did Doc give you a key?"

"Yes. Why? What kind of a yarn is he feeding *you?*"

"Bring down the key, Rance. Quick."

He looked back over his shoulder again, started toward me, and then hesitated. He compromised by staying where he was, but watching me.

The window slammed down.

I walked back around the car and I almost decided to light a match and look at those stains myself. And then I decided, what the hell.

Hank came a few steps closer. He said, "Where you going, Doc?"

I was at the kerb by then, I said, "Nowhere", and sat down.

To wait.

CHAPTER TWELVE

Then fill up the glasses as quick as you can,
And sprinkle the table with buttons and bran:
Put cats in the coffee, and mice in the tea—
And welcome Queen Alice with thirty-times-three!

THE courthouse door opened and closed. Kates crossed the street. He looked at me and asked Hank, "What's wrong?"

"Don't know, Rance. Looks like blood has dripped from the luggage compartment of Doc's car. It's locked. He says he gave you the key. I didn't want to—uh—leave him to come up and get it. So I yelled for you."

Kates nodded. His face was toward me and Hank Ganzer couldn't see it. I could. It looked happy, very happy.

His hand went inside his coat and came out with a pistol. He asked, "Did you frisk him, Hank?"

"No."

"Go ahead."

Hank came around Kates and came up to me from the side. I stood up and held out my hands to make it easy for him. The bottle of whisky was in one of them. He found nothing more deadly than that.

"Clean," Hank said.

Kates didn't put his pistol away. He reached into a pocket with his free hand and took out the key I'd given him. He tossed it to Hank. "Open the compartment," he said.

The key fitted. The handle turned. Hank lifted the door.

I heard the sudden intake of his breath and I turned and looked. Two bodies; I could see that much. I couldn't tell who they were from where I stood. Hank leaned farther in, using his flashlight.

He said, "Miles Harrison, Rance. And Ralph Bonney. Both dead."

"How'd he kill 'em?"

"Hit over the head with something. Hard. Must've been several blows apiece. There's lots of blood."

"Weapon there?"

"What looks like it. There's a revolver—an old one—with blood on the butt. Nickel-plated Iver-Johnson, rusty where the plating's off. Thirty-eight, I think."

"The money there? The pay roll?"

"There's what looks like a brief case under Miles." Hank turned around. His face was as pale as the starlight. "Do I got to—uh—move him, Rance?"

Kates thought a minute. "Maybe we better not. Maybe we better take a photo first. Listen, Hank, you go upstairs and get that camera and flashgun. And while you're there, phone Dr. Heil to get here right away. Uh—you're sure they're both dead?"

"Christ yes, Rance. Their heads are beaten in. Shall I call Dorberg, too?" Dorberg is the local mortician who gets whatever business the sheriff's office can throw his way; he's Kates' brother-in-law, which may have a bearing on the fact.

Kates said, "Sure, tell him to bring the wagon. But tell him no hurry; we want the coroner to have a look before we move 'em. And we want the pix even before that."

Hank started for the courthouse door and then turned again. "Uh—Rance, how about calling Miles' wife and Bonney's factory?"

I sat down on the kerb again. I wanted a drink more badly than before, and the bottle was in my hand. But it didn't seem right, just at that moment, to take one. Miles' wife, I thought, and Bonney's factory. What a hell of a difference that was. But Bonney had been divorced that very day; he had no children, no relatives at all—at least in Carmel City—that I knew of. But then I didn't have either. If I was murdered, who'd be notified? The *Carmel City Clarion,* and maybe Carl Trenholm, if whoever did the notifying knew that Trenholm was my closest friend. Yes, maybe on the whole it was better that I'd never married. I thought of Bonney's divorce and the facts behind it that Carl—through Smiley—had told me. And I thought of how Miles Harrison's wife would be feeling tonight as soon as she got the news. But that was different; I didn't know whether it was good or bad that nobody would feel that way about me if I died suddenly.

Just the same I felt lonely as hell. Well, they'd arrest me now and that would mean I could call Carl as my attorney. I was going to be in a hell of a spot, but Carl would believe me—and believe that I was sane—if anybody would.

Kates had been thinking. He said, "Not yet—either of them, Hank. Milly especially; she might rush down here and get here before we got the bodies to Dorberg's. And we might as well be able to tell the factory whether the pay roll's there when we phone them. Maybe Stoeger hid it somewhere else and we won't get it back tonight."

Hank said, "That's right, about Milly. We wouldn't want her to see Miles—that way. Okay, so I'll call Heil and Dorberg and then come back with the camera."

"Quit talking. Get going."

Hank went on into the courthouse.

It wasn't any use, but I had to say it. I said. "Listen, Kates, I didn't do that. I didn't kill them."

Kates said, "You son of a bitch. Miles was a good guy."

"He was. I didn't kill him." I thought, I wish Miles had let me buy him that drink early in the evening. I wish I'd known; I'd have insisted and talked him into it. But that was silly, of course; you can't know things in advance. If you could, you could stop them happening. Except of course in the Looking-Glass country where people sometimes lived backwards, where the White Queen had screamed first and then later had stuck the needle into her finger. But even then—except, of course, that the Alice books were merely delightful nonsense—why hadn't she simply not picked up the needle she knew she was going to stick herself with?

Delightful nonsense, that is, until tonight. Tonight somebody was making gibbering horror out of Lewis Carroll's most amusing episodes. "Drink Me"—and die suddenly and horribly. That key—it had been supposed to open a fifteen-inch-high door into a beautiful garden. What it had opened the door to—well, I didn't care to look.

I sighed and thought, what the hell, it's over with now. I'm going to be arrested and Kates thinks I killed Miles and Bonney, but I can't blame him for thinking it. I've got to wait till Carl can get me out of this.

Kates said, "Stand up, Stoeger."

I didn't. Why should I? I'd just thought, why would Miles or Ralph mind if I took a drink out of this bottle in my hand? I started to unscrew the top.

"Stand up, Stoeger. Or I'll shoot you right there."

He *meant* it. I stood up. His face, as he stood then, was in the shadow, but I remembered that look of malevolence he'd given me in his office, the look that said, "I'd like to kill you."

He was going to shoot me. Here and now.

It was safe as houses for him to do so. He could claim—if I turned and ran and he shot me in the back—that he'd shot because I was trying to escape. And if from the front that I—a homicidal maniac who had already killed Miles and Bonney—was coming toward him to attack him.

That was why he'd sent Hank away and given him two phone calls to make so he wouldn't be back for minutes.

I said, "Kates, you're not serious. You wouldn't shoot a man down in cold blood."

"A man who'd killed a deputy of mine, yes. If I don't, Stoeger, you might beat the rap. You might get certified as a looney and get away with it. I'll make sure." That wasn't all of it, of course, but it gave him an excuse to help his own conscience. I'd killed a deputy of his, he'd thought. But he'd hated me enough to want to kill me even before he'd thought that. Hatred and sadism—given a perfect excuse.

What could I do? Yell? It wouldn't help. Probably nobody awake—it was well after three o'clock by now—would hear me in time to see what happened. Hank would be phoning in the back office; he wouldn't get to the window in time.

And Kates would claim that I yelled as I jumped him; yelling would just trigger the gun.

He stepped closer; if he shot me in the front there'd have to be powder marks to show that he'd shot while I was coming at him. The gun muzzle centred on my chest, barely a foot away. I could live seconds longer if I turned and ran; he'd probably wait until I was a dozen steps away in that case.

His face was still in the shadow, but I could see that he was grinning. I couldn't see his eyes or most of the rest of his face, just the grin. A disembodied grin, like that of the Cheshire cat in Alice. But unlike the Cheshire cat, he wasn't going to fade away.

I was. Unless something unexpected happened. Like maybe a witness coming along, over there on the opposite sidewalk. He wouldn't shoot me in cold blood before a witness. Carl Trenholm, Al Grainger, anybody.

I looked over Kates' shoulder and called out, "Hi, Al!"

Kates turned. He had to; he couldn't take a chance on the possibility that there was really someone coming.

He turned his head just for a quick glance, to be sure.

I swung the whisky bottle. Maybe I should say my hand swung it; I hadn't even remembered that I still held it. It hit Kates alongside the head and like as not the brim of his hat saved his life. I think I swung hard enough to have killed him if he'd been bare headed.

Kates and the revolver he'd been holding hit the street, separately. The whisky bottle slid out of my hand and hit the paving; it broke. The paving must have been harder than Kates' head—or maybe it would have broken on Kates' head if it hadn't been for the brim of his hat.

I didn't even stop to find out if he was dead. I ran like hell.

Afoot, of course. The ignition key of my car was still in my pocket, but driving off with two corpses was just about the last thing in the world I wanted to do.

I ran a block and winded myself before I realized I hadn't the faintest idea where I was going. I slowed down and got off Oak Street. I cut back into the first alley. I fell over a garbage can and then sat down on it to get my wind back and to think out what I was going to do. But I had to move on because a dog started barking.

I found myself behind the courthouse.

I wanted, of course, to know who had killed Ralph Bonney and Miles Harrison and put their bodies in my car, but there was something that seemed of even more immediate interest; I wanted to know if I'd killed Rance Kates or seriously injured him. If I had, I was in a hell of a jam because—in addition to everything else against me—it would be my word against his that I'd done it in self-defence, to save my own life. My word against his, that is, if he were only injured. My word against nothing at all if I'd killed him.

And my word wouldn't mean a damn thing to anybody until and unless I could account for two corpses in my car.

The first window I tried was unlocked. I guess they're careless about locking windows of the courthouse because, for one reason, there's nothing kept there that any ordinary burglar would want to steal, and for another reason because the sheriff's office is in the building, and somebody's on duty there all night long.

I slid the window up very slowly and it didn't make much noise, not enough, anyway, to have been heard in the sheriffs office, which is on the second floor and near the front. I put it down again, just as quietly, so it wouldn't be an open give-away if the search for me went through the alley.

I groped in the dark till I found a chair and sat down to collect what wits I had left and figure what to do next. I was fairly safe for the moment. The room I'd entered was one of the small anterooms off the court-room; nobody would look for me here, as long as I kept quiet.

They'd found the sheriff all right, or the sheriff had come around and found himself. There were footsteps on the front stairs, footsteps of more than one person. But back here I was too far away to hear what was being said, if any talking was going on.

But that could wait for a minute or two.

I wished to hell that I had a drink; I'd never wanted one worse in my life. I cussed myself for having dropped and broken that bottle—and after it had saved my life, at that. If I hadn't happened to have it in my hand, I'd have been dead.

I don't know how long I sat there, but it probably wasn't over a few minutes because I was still breathing a little hard when I decided I'd better move. If I'd had a bottle to keep me company, I'd have gladly sat there the rest of the night, I think.

But I had to find out what happened to Kates. If I'd killed him—or if he'd been taken to the hospital and was out of the picture—then I'd better give myself up and get it over with. If he was all right, and was still running things, that wouldn't be a very smart thing to do. If he'd wanted to kill me before I'd knocked him out with that bottle, he'd want to do it so badly now that he would do it, maybe without even bothering to find an excuse, right in front of Hank or any of the other deputies who were undoubtedly being woken up to join the manhunt, in front of the coroner or anybody else who happened to be around.

I bent down and took my shoes off before I got up. I put one in each of the side pockets of my coat and then tiptoed out through the courtroom to the back stairs. I'd been in the building so many thousand times that I knew the layout almost as well as that of my own home or the *Clarion* office, and I didn't run into anything or fall over anything.

I guided myself up the dark back staircase with a hand on the banister and avoiding the middle of the steps, where they'd be most likely to creak.

Luckily there is an el in the upstairs hallway that runs from the front stairs to the back ones so there wasn't any danger of my being seen, when I'd reached the top of the stairs, by anyone entering or leaving the sheriffs office. And I had dim light now, from the light in the front hallway near the sheriff's office door.

I tiptoed along almost to the turn of the hall and then tried the door of the county surveyor's office, which is next to the sheriff's office and with only an ordinary door with a ground glass pane between them. The door was unlocked.

I got it open very quietly. It slipped out of my hand when I started to close it from the inside and almost slammed, but I caught it in time and eased it shut. I would have liked to lock it, but I didn't know whether the lock would click or not, so I didn't take a chance on that.

I had plenty of light, comparatively, in the surveyor's office; the ground glass pane of the door to the sheriff's office was a bright yellow rectangle through which came enough light to let me see the office furniture clearly. I avoided it carefully and tiptoed my way toward that yellow rectangle.

I could hear voices now and as I neared the door I could hear them even better, but I couldn't quite make out whose they were or what they were saying until I put my ear against the glass. I could hear perfectly well, then.

Hank Ganzer was saying, "It still throws me, Rance. A gentle little old guy like Doc. Two murders and——"

"Gentle, hell!" It was Kates' voice. "Maybe when he was sane he was, but he's crazier than a bedbug now. Ow! Go easy with that tape, will you?"

Dr. Heil's voice was soft, harder to understand. He seemed to be urging that Kates should let himself be taken to the hospital to be sure there wasn't any concussion.

"The hell with that," Kates said. "Not till we get Stoeger before he kills anybody else. Like he killed Miles and Bonney and damn near killed me. Hank, what's about the bodies?"

"I made a quick preliminary examination." Heil's voice was clearer now. "Cause of death is pretty obviously repeated blows on their heads with what seems to have been that rusty pistol on your desk. And with the stains on the pistol butt, I don't think there's any reason to doubt it."

"They still out front?"

Hank said, "No, they're at Dorberg's—or on their way there. He and one of his boys came around with his meat wagon."

"Doc." It was Kates' voice and it made me jump a little until I realized that he was talking to Dr. Heil and not to me. "You about through? With that God damn bandage, I mean. I got to get going on this. Hank, how many of the boys did you get on the phone? How many are coming down?"

"Three, Rance. I got Watkins, Ehlers and Bill Dean. They're all on their way down. Be here in a few minutes. That'll make five of us."

"Guess that fixes up things as well as I can here, Rance," Dr. Heil's voice said. "I still suggest you go around to the hospital for an X-ray and a check-up as soon as you can."

"Sure, Doc. Soon as I catch Stoeger. And he can't get out of town with the state police watching the roads for us, even if he steals a car. You go on around to Dorberg's and take care of things there, huh?"

Heil's voice, soft again, said something I couldn't hear, and there were footsteps toward the outer hall. I could hear other footsteps coming up the stairs. One or more of the day-shift deputies were arriving.

Kates said, "Hi, Bill, Walt. Ehlers with you?"

"Didn't see him. Probably be here in a minute." It sounded like Bill Dean's voice.

"That's all right. We'll leave him here, anyway. You both got your guns? Good. Listen, you two are going together and Hank and I are going together. We'll work in pairs. Don't worry about the roads leading out; the state boys are watching them for us. And there's no train or bus out till late tomorrow morning. We just comb the town."

"Divide it between us, Rance?"

"No. You, Walt and Bill cover the whole town. Drive through every street and alley. Hank and I will take places he might have holed in to hide. We'll search his house and the *Clarion* office, whether there are lights on or not, and we'll try any place else that's indoors where he might've holed in. He might pick an empty house, for instance. Anybody got any other suggestions where he might think of holing in?"

Bill Dean's voice said, "He's pretty thick with Carl Trenholm. He might go to Carl."

"Good idea, Bill. Anybody else?"

Hank said, "He looked pretty drunk to me. And he broke that bottle he had. Might get into his head he wants another drink and break into a tavern. Probably Smiley's; that's where he hangs out, mostly."

"Okay, Hank. We'll check—— That must be Dick coming. Any more ideas, anybody, before we split up?"

Ehlers was coming in now. Hank said, "Sometimes a guy doubles back where he figures nobody'll figure where he is. I mean, Rance, maybe he doubled back here and got in the back way or something, thinking the safest place to hide's right under our noses. Right here in the building."

Kates said, "You heard that, Dick. And you're staying here to watch the office, so that's your job. Search the building here first before you settle down."

"Right, Rance."

Kates said, "One more thing. He's dangerous. He's probably armed by now. So don't take any chances. When you see him, start shooting."

"At Doc Stoeger?" Someone's voice sounded surprised and a little shocked. I couldn't tell which of the deputies it was.

"At Doc Stoeger," Kates said. "Maybe you think of him as a harmless little guy—but that's the kind that generally makes homicidal maniacs. He's killed two men tonight and tried to kill me, probably thought he did kill me, or he'd have stayed and finished the job. And don't forget who one of the men he did kill was. Miles."

Somebody muttered something.

Bill Dean—I think it was Bill Dean—said, "I don't get it, though. A guy like Doc. He isn't broke; he's got a paper that makes money and he's not a crook. Why'd he suddenly want to kill two men for a couple of thousand lousy bucks?"

Kates swore. He said, "He's nuts, went off the beam. The money probably didn't have much to do with it, although he took it all right. It was in that brief case under Miles' body. Now listen, this is the last time I tell you; he's a homicidal maniac and you better remember Miles the minute you spot him and shoot quick. He's crazy as a bedbug. Came in here with a cock and bull story about a guy being croaked out at the Wentworth place—a guy named Yehudi Smith, of all names. And Doc had a card to prove it, only he printed the card himself. Crazy enough to put his own bug number—union label number—on it. Gives me a key that he says opens a fifteen-inch-high door to a beautiful garden. Well, that was the key to the luggage compartment of his own car, see? With Miles' and Bonney's bodies, and the pay roll money, in it. Parked right in front. He'd driven it here. Comes up and *gives me the key*. And tries to get me to go to a haunted house with him."

"Did anybody look there?" Dean asked.

Hank said, "Sure, Bill. On my way back from Neilsville. Went through the whole dump. Nothing. And listen, Rance is right about him being crazy. I heard some of the stuff he said, myself. And if you don't think he's dangerous, look at Rance. I'm sorry about it, I liked Doc. But damn it, I'm with Rance on shooting first and catching him afterwards."

Somebody: "God damn it, if he killed Miles——"

"If he's *that crazy*"—I think it was Dick Ehlers—"we'd be doing him a favour, the way I figure it. If *I* ever got that far off the beam, homicidal, damn if I wouldn't rather be shot than spend the rest of my life in a padded cell. But what *made* him go off that way? All of a sudden, I mean?"

"Alcohol. Softens the brain, and then all of a sudden, whang."

"Doc didn't drink that much. He'd get drunk, a little, a night or two a week; but he wasn't an alcoholic. And he was such a nice——'

A fist hit a desk. It would have been Kates' fist and Kates' desk. It was Kates' swivel chair that squealed and his voice that said, "What the hell are we having a sewing circle for. Come on, let's go out and get him. And about shooting first, that's *orders*. I've lost one deputy tonight already. Come on."

Footsteps, lots of them, toward the door.

Kates' voice calling back from it, "And don't forget to search this building, Dick. Cellar to roof, before you settle down here."

"Right, Rance."

Footsteps, lots of heavy footsteps, going down the steps. And one set of them turning back along the hallway.

Toward the County Surveyor's office.

Toward me.

CHAPTER THIRTEEN

And he was very proud and stiff:
He said "I'd go and wake them, if——"
I took a corkscrew from the shelf:
I went to wake them up myself.

I HOPED he'd take Rance Kates' orders literally and search the place from cellar to attic, in that order. If he did, I could get out either the front or back way while he was in the basement. But he might start on this floor, with this room.

So I tiptoed to the door, pulling one of my shoes out of my pocket as I went. I stood flat against the wall by the door, gripping the shoe, ready to swing the heel of it if Ehler's head came in.

It didn't. The footsteps went on past and started down the back staircase. I breathed again.

I opened the door and stepped out into the hall as soon as the footsteps were at the bottom of the back steps. Out there in the hall, in the quiet of the night, I could hear him moving about down there. He didn't go to the basement; he was taking the main floor first. That wasn't good. With him on the first floor I couldn't risk either the front or the back stairs; I was stuck up here.

Outside I heard first one car start and then another. At least the front entrance was clear if I had to try to leave that way, if Ehlers started upstairs by the back staircase.

I took a spot in the middle of the hallway, equidistant from both flights of steps. I could still hear him walking around down on the floor below, but it was difficult to tell just where he was. I had to be ready to make a break in either direction.

I swore to myself at the thoroughness of Kates' plans for finding me. My house, my office, Carl's place, Smiley's or another tavern—every place I'd actually be likely to go. Even here, the courthouse, where I really was. But luckily, instead of all of them pitching in for a quick once-over here, he'd left only one man to do the job, and as long as I could hear him and he couldn't hear me—and probably didn't believe I was really here at all—I had an edge.

Only, damn it, why didn't Ehlers hurry? I wanted a drink, and if I could get out of here, I could get one somewhere somehow. I was shaking like a leaf, and my thoughts were, too. Even one drink would steady me enough to think straight.

Maybe Kates kept a bottle in the bottom drawer of his desk.

The way I felt just then, it was worth trying. I listened hard to the sounds below me and decided Ehlers was probably at the back of the building and I tiptoed to the front and into Kates' office.

I went back to his desk and pulled the drawer open very quietly and slowly. There was a whisky bottle there. It was empty.

I cussed Kates under my breath. It wasn't bad enough that he'd tried to kill me; on top of that, he'd had to finish off that bottle without leaving a single drink in it. And it had been a good brand, too.

I closed the drawer again as carefully as I'd opened it, so there'd be no sign of my having been there.

Lying on the blotter on Kates' desk was a revolver. I looked at it, wondering whether I should take it along with me. For a second the fact that it was rusty didn't register and then I remembered Hank's description of the gun that had been used as a bludgeon to kill Miles and Bonney, and I bent closer. Yes, it was an Iver-Johnson, nickel-plated where the plating wasn't worn or knocked off. This was the death weapon, then.

Exhibit A.

I reached out to pick it up, and then jerked my hand back. Hadn't I been framed well enough without helping the framer by putting my fingerprints on that gun? That was all I needed, to have my fingerprints on the weapon that had done the killing. Or were they there already? Considering everything else, I wouldn't have been too surprised if they were.

Then I almost went through the ceiling. The phone rang.

I could hear, in the silence between the first ring and the second, Ehler's footsteps starting upstairs. But back here in the office, I couldn't tell whether he was coming up the front way or the back, and I might not have time to make it anyway, even if I knew.

I looked around frantically and saw a closet, the door ajar. I grabbed up the Iver-Johnson and ducked into the closet, behind the door. And I stood there, trying not to breathe, while Ehlers came in and picked up the phone.

He said, "Sheriff's office," and then, "Oh you, Rance," and then he listened a while.

"You're phoning from the *Clarion?* Not at Smiley's or there, huh? . . . No, no calls have come in. . . . Yeah, I'm almost through looking around here. Searched the first floor and the basement. Just got to go over this floor yet."

I swore at myself. He'd been down in the basement then, and I could have got away. But the building had been so quiet that his walking around down there had sounded to me as though it had been on the main floor.

'Don't worry, I'm not taking any chances, Rance. Gun in one hand and a flashlight in the other."

There was a gun in my hand, too, and suddenly I realized what a damned foolish thing I'd done to pick it up off Kates' desk. Ehlers must have known it was there. If he missed it, if he happened to glance down at the desk while he was talking on the phone—

God must have loved me. He didn't. He said, "Okay, Rance," and then he put the phone down and walked out.

I heard him go back along the hallway and around the el and start opening doors back there. I had to get out quick, down the front steps, before he worked his way back here. As a matter of routine, he'd probably open this closet door too when he'd searched his way back to the office he'd started from.

I let myself out and tiptoed down the steps. Out into the night again, on to Oak Street. And I had to get off it quick, because either of the two cars looking for me might cruise by at any moment. Carmel City isn't large; a car can cruise all of its streets and alleys in pretty short order.

Besides I still had my shoes in my pockets and—I realized now—I still had a gun in my hand.

Hoping Ehlers wouldn't happen to be looking out of any of the windows, I ran around the corner and into the mouth of the alley behind the courthouse. As soon as I was comparatively safe in the friendly darkness, I sat down on the alley kerbstone and put my shoes back on, and put the gun into my pocket. I hadn't meant to bring it along at all, but as long as I had I couldn't throw it away now.

Anyway, it was going to get Dick Ehlers in trouble with Kates. When Kates looked for that gun and found it missing, he'd know that I'd been in the courthouse and that Ehlers had missed me. He'd know that I'd been right in his own office while he'd been out searching for me.

And so there I was in the dark, in safety for a few minutes until a car full of deputies decided to cruise down that particular alley looking for me. And I had a gun in my pocket that might or might not shoot—I hadn't checked that—and I had my shoes on and my hands were shaking again.

I didn't even have to ask myself, '*Little man, what now?*' The little man not only wanted a drink; he really needed one.

And Kates had already been to Smiley's looking for me and had found that I wasn't there.

So I started down the alley toward Smiley's.

Funny, but I was getting over being scared. A little, anyway. You can get only just *so* scared, and then something happens to your adrenal glands or something. I can't remember offhand whether your adrenals make you frightened or whether they get going and operate against it, but mine were getting either into or out of action, as the case might be. I'd been scared so much that night that I—or my glands—was getting tired of it.

I was getting brave, almost. And it wasn't Dutch courage, either; it had been so long since I'd had a drink that I'd forgotten what one tasted like. I was cold damn sober. About three times during the course of the long evening and the long night I'd been on the borderline of intoxication, but always something had happened to keep me from drinking for a while and then something had sobered me up. Some foolish little thing like being taken for a ride by gangsters or watching a man die suddenly or horribly by quaffing a bottle labelled "Drink Me" or finding murdered men in the back of my own car or discovering that a sheriff intended to shoot me down in cold blood. Little things like that.

So I kept going down the alley toward Smiley's. The dog that had barked at me before barked again. But I didn't waste time barking back. I kept on going down the alley toward Smiley's.

There was the street to cross. I took a quick look both ways but didn't worry about it beyond that. If the sheriff's car or the deputies' car suddenly turned the corner and started spraying me with headlights and then bullets, well, then that was that. You can only get so worried; then you quit worrying. When things can't get any worse, outside of your getting killed, then either you get killed or things start getting better.

Things started to get better; the window into the back room of Smiley's was open. I didn't bother taking off my shoes this time. Smiley would be asleep upstairs, but alone, and Smiley's so sound a sleeper that a bazooka shell exploding in the next room wouldn't wake him. I remember times I've dropped into the tavern on a dull afternoon and found him asleep; it was almost hopeless to try to wake him, and I'd generally help myself and leave the money on the ledge of the register. And he dropped asleep so quickly and easily that even if Kates and Hank had wakened him when they'd look for me here, he'd be asleep again by now.

In fact—yes, I could hear a faint rumbling sound overhead, like very distant thunder. Smiley snoring.

I groped my way through the dark back room and opened the door to the tavern. There was a dim light in there that burned all night long, and the shades were left up. But Kates had already been here and the chances of anyone else happening to pass and look in at half-past three of a Friday morning were negligible.

I took a bottle of the best bonded Bourbon Smiley had from the back bar and because it looked as though there was still at least a fair chance that this might be the last drink I ever had, I took a bottle of seltzer from the case under the bar. I took them to the table around the el, the one that's out of sight of the windows, the table at which Bat and George had sat early this evening.

Bat and George seemed, now, to have sat there a long time ago, years maybe, and seemed not a tenth as frightening as they'd been at the time. Almost, they seemed a little funny, somehow.

I left the two bottles on the table and went back for a glass, a swizzle stick, and some ice cubes from the refrigerator. This drink I'd waited a long time for, and it was going to be a good one.

I'd even pay a good price for it, I decided, especially after I looked in my wallet and found I had several tens but nothing smaller. I put a ten-dollar bill on the ledge of the register, and I wondered if I'd ever get my change out of it.

I went back to the table and made myself a drink, a good one.

I lighted up a cigar, too. That was a bit risky because if Kates came by here again for another check, he might see cigar smoke in the dim light, even though I was out of his range of vision. But I decided the risk was worth it. You can, I was finding, get into such a God-awful jam that a little more risk doesn't seem to matter at all.

I took a long good swig of the drink and then a deep drag from the cigar, and I felt pretty good. I held out my hands and they weren't shaking. Very silly of them not to be, but they weren't.

Now, I thought, is my first chance to think for a long time. My first real chance since Yehudi Smith had died.

Little man, what now?

The pattern. Could I make any sense out of the pattern?

Yehudi Smith—only that undoubtedly wasn't his real name, else the card he gave me wouldn't have been printed in my own shop—had called to see me and had told me——

Skip what he told you, I told myself. That was gobbledegook, just the kind of gobbledegook that would entice you to go to such a crazy place at such a crazy time. He knew you—that is, I corrected myself—he knew a lot about you. Your hobby and your weaknesses and what you were and what would interest you.

His coming there was planned. Planned well in advance; the card proved that.

According to a plan, he called on you at a time when no one else would be there. Probably, sitting in his car, he'd watched you come home, knowing Mrs. Carr was there—in all probability he or someone had been watching the house all evening—and waiting until she'd left to present himself.

No one had seen him, no one besides yourself.

He'd led you on a wild-goose chase. There weren't any Vorpal Blades; that was gobbledegook, too.

Connect that with the fact that Miles Harrison and Ralph Bonney had been killed while Yehudi Smith was keeping you entertained and busy, and that their bodies had been put in the back compartment of your car.

Easy. Smith was an accomplice of the murderer, hired to keep you away from anybody else who might alibi you while the crime was going on. Also to give you such an incredible story to account for where you really were that your own mother, if she were still alive, would have a hard time believing it.

But connect that with the fact that Smith had been killed, too. And with the fact that the pay roll money had been left in your car along with the bodies.

It added up to gibberish.

I took another sip of my drink and it tasted weak. I looked at it and saw I'd been sitting there so long between sips that most of the ice had melted. I put more of the bonded Bourbon in it and it tasted all right again.

I remembered about the gun I'd grabbed up from Kates' desk, the rusty one with which the two murders had been committed. I took it out of my pocket and looked at it. I handled it so I wouldn't have to touch their dried stains on the butt.

I broke it to see if any shots had been fired from it and found there weren't any cartridges in it, empty or otherwise. I clicked it back into position and tried the trigger. It was rusted shut. It hadn't, then, been used as a gun at all. Just as a hammer to bash out the brains of two men.

And I'd certainly made a fool of myself by bringing it along. I'd played right into the killer's hands by doing that. I put it back into my pocket.

I wished that I had someone to talk to. I felt that I might figure out things aloud better than I could this way. I wished that Smiley was awake, and for a moment I was tempted to go upstairs to get him. No, I decided, once already tonight I'd put Smiley in danger—danger out of which he'd got both of us and without any help from me whatsoever.

And this was *my* problem. It wouldn't be fair to Smiley to tangle him in it.

Besides, this wasn't a matter for Smiley's brawn and guts. This was like playing chess, and Smiley didn't play chess. Carl might possibly be able to help me figure it out, but Smiley—never. And I didn't want to tangle Carl in this either.

But I wanted to *talk* to somebody.

All right, maybe I was a little crazy—not drunk, definitely not drunk—but a little crazy. I wanted to talk to somebody, so I did.

The little man who wasn't there.

I imagined him sitting across the table from me, sitting there with an imaginary drink in his hand. Gladly, right gladly, would I have poured him a real one if he'd been really there. He was looking at me strangely.

"Smitty," I said.

"Yes, Doc?"

"What's your real name, Smitty? I know it *isn't* Yehudi Smith. That was part of the gag. The card you gave me proves that."

It wasn't the right question to ask. He wavered a little, as though he was going to disappear on me. I shouldn't have asked him a question that I myself couldn't answer, because he was there only because my mind was putting him there. He couldn't tell me anything I didn't know myself or couldn't figure out.

He wavered a little, but he rallied. He said, "Doc, I can't tell you that. Any more than I can tell you whom I was working for. You know that."

Get it; he said "whom I was working for" not "who I was working for." I felt proud of him and of myself.

I said, "Sure, Smitty. I shouldn't have asked. And listen, I'm sorry—I'm sorry as hell that you died."

"That's all right, Doc. We all die sometime. And—well, it was a nice evening up to then."

"I'm glad I fed you," I said. "I'm glad I gave you all you wanted to drink. And listen, Smitty, I'm sorry I laughed out loud when I saw that bottle and key on the glass-topped table. I just couldn't help it. It *was* funny."

"Sure, Doc. But I had to play it straight. It was part of the act. But it was corny; I don't blame you for acting amused. And, Doc, I'm sorry I did it. I didn't know the whole score—you've got proof of that. If I had,

136

I wouldn't have drunk what was in that bottle. I didn't look like a man who wanted to die, did I, Doc?"

I shook my head slowly, looking at the laughter-lines around his eyes and his mouth. He didn't look like a man who wanted to die.

But he had died, suddenly and horribly.

"I'm sorry, Smitty," I told him. "I'm sorry as hell. I'd give a hell of a lot to bring you back, to have you really sitting there."

He chuckled. "Don't get maudlin, Doc. It'll spoil your thinking. You're trying to think, you know."

"I know," I said. "But I had to get it out of my system. All right, Smitty. You're dead and I can't do anything about it. You're the little man who isn't there. And I can't ask you any questions I can't answer myself, so really you can't help me."

"Are you sure, Doc? Even if you ask the right questions?"

"What do you mean? That my subconscious mind might know the answers even if I don't?"

He laughed. "Let's not get Freudian. Let's stick to Lewis Carroll. I really *was* a Carroll enthusiast, you know. I was a fast study, but not that fast. I couldn't have memorized all that about him just for one occasion."

The phrase struck me, "a fast study." I repeated it and went on where it led me. "You were an actor, Smitty? Hell, don't answer it. You must have been. I should have guessed that. An actor hired to play a part."

He grinned a bit wryly. "Not too good an actor, then, or you wouldn't have guessed it. And pretty much of a sucker, Doc, to have accepted the role. I should have guessed that there was more in it than what he told me." He shrugged. "Well, I played you a dirty trick, but I played a worse one on myself. Didn't I?"

"I'm sorry you're dead, Smitty. God damn it, I *liked* you."

"I'm glad, Doc. I haven't liked myself too well these last few years. You've figured it out by now so I can tell you—I was pretty down and out to take a booking like that, and at the price he offered me for it. And, damn him, he didn't pay me in advance except my expenses, so what did I gain by it? I got killed. Wait, don't get maudlin about that again. Let's drink to it."

We drank to it. There are worse things than getting killed. And there are worse ways of dying than suddenly when you aren't expecting it, when you're slightly tight and———

But that subject wasn't getting us anywhere.

"You were a character actor," I said.

"Doc, you disappoint me by belaboring the obvious. And that doesn't help you to figure out who Anybody is."

"Anybody?"

"That's what you were calling him to yourself when you were thinking things out, in a half-witted sort of way, not so long ago. Remember thinking that Anybody could have got into your printing shop and Anybody could have set up one line of type and figured out how to print one good card on that little hand press, but why would Anybody———"

"Unfair," I said. "You can get inside my mind, because—because, hell, that's where you *are*. But I can't get into yours. You know who Anybody is. But I don't."

"Even I, Doc, might not know his real name. In case something went wrong, he wouldn't have told me that. Something like—well, suppose you'd grabbed that 'DRINK ME' bottle when you first found the table and tossed it off before I could tell you that it was my prerogative to do so. Yes, there were a lot of things that could have gone wrong in so complicated a deal as that one was."

I nodded. "Yes, suppose Al Grainger had come around for that game of chess and we'd taken him along. Suppose—suppose I hadn't lived to get home at all. I had a narrow squeak earlier in the evening, you know."

"In that case, Doc, it never would have happened. You ought to be able to figure that out without my telling you. If you'd been killed, you and Smiley, earlier in the evening, then—at least if Anybody had learned about it, as he probably would have—Ralph Bonney and Miles Harrison wouldn't have been killed later. At least not tonight. A wheel would have come off the plans and I'd have gone back to—wherever I came from. And everything would have been off."

I said, "But suppose I'd stayed at the office far into the night working on one of those big stories I thought I had—and was so happy about. How would Anybody have known?"

"Can't tell you that, Doc. But you might guess. Suppose I had orders to keep Anybody posted on your movements, if they went off schedule. When you left the house, saying you'd be back shortly, I'd have used your phone and told him that. And when you phoned that you were on your way back I'd have let him know, while you were walking home, wouldn't I?"

"But that was pretty late."

"Not too late for him to have intercepted Miles Harrison and Ralph Bonney on their way back from Neilsville—under certain circumstances—if his plans had been held in abeyance until he was sure you'd be home and out of circulation before midnight."

I said, "Under certain circumstances," and wondered just what I meant by it.

Yehudi Smith smiled. He lifted his glass and looked at me mockingly over the rim of it before he drank. He said, "Go on, Doc. You're only in the second square, but your next move will be a good one. You go to the fourth square by train, you know."

"And the smoke alone is worth a thousand pounds a puff."

"And that's the answer, Doc," he said, quietly.

I stared at him. A prickle went down my back.

Outside, in the night, a clock struck four times.

"What do you mean, Smitty?" I asked him slowly.

The little man who wasn't there poured more whisky from an imaginary bottle into his imaginary glass. He said, "Doc, you've been letting the glass-topped table and the bottle and the key fool you. They're from *Alice in Wonderland*. Originally, of course, called *Alice's Adventures Underground*. Wonderful book. But you're in the second."

"The second square? You just said that."

"The second book. *Through the Looking-Glass, and What Alice Found There.* And, Doc, you know as well as I what Alice found there."

I poured myself another drink, a short one this time, to match his. I didn't bother with ice or seltzer.

He raised his glass. "You've got it now, Doc," he said. "Not all of it, but enough to start on. You might still see the dawn come up."

"Don't be so God damn dramatic," I said; "certainly I'm going to see the dawn come up."

139

"Even if Kates comes here again looking for you? Don't forget when he misses that rusty gun in your pocket, he'll know you were at the courthouse when he was looking for you here. He might recheck all his previous stops. And you're awfully damned careless in filling the place with cigar smoke, you know."

"You mean it's worth a thousand pounds a puff?"

He put back his head and laughed and then he quit laughing and he wasn't there any more, even in my imagination, because a sudden slight sound made me look toward the door that led upstairs, to Smiley's rooms. The door opened and Smiley was standing there.

In a nightshirt. I hadn't known anybody wore nightshirts any more, but Smiley wore one. His eyes looked sleepy and his hair—what was left of it—was tousled and he was barefoot. He had a gun in his hand, the little short-barrelled thirty-eight Banker's Special I'd given him some hours ago. In his huge hand it looked tiny, a toy. It didn't look like something that had knocked a Buick off the road, killing one man and badly injuring another, that very evening.

There wasn't any expression on his face, none at all.

I wonder what mine looked like. But through a looking-glass or not, I didn't have one to look into.

Had I been talking to myself aloud? Or had my conversation with Yehudi Smith been imaginary, within my own mind? I honestly didn't know.

If I'd really been talking to myself, it was going to be a hell of a thing to have to explain. Especially if Kates had, on his stop here, awakened Smiley and told him that I was crazy.

In any case, what the hell could I possibly say right now but "Hello, Smiley?"

I opened my mouth to say "Hello, Smiley," but I didn't.

Someone was pounding on the glass of the front door. Someone who yelled, "Hey, open up here!" in the voice of Sheriff Rance Kates.

I did the only reasonable thing to do. I poured myself another drink.

CHAPTER FOURTEEN

"You are old," said the youth," one would hardly suppose
That your eye was as steady as ever;
Yet you balanced an eel on the end of your nose——
What made you so awfully clever?"

KATES hammered again and tried the knob.

Smiley stared at me and I stared back at him. I couldn't say anything—
even if I could have thought of anything to say—to him at that distance
without the probability of Kates hearing my voice.

Kates hammered again. I heard him say something to Hank about
breaking in the glass. Smiley bent down and placed the gun on the step
behind him and then came out of the door into the tavern. Without
looking at me he walked toward the front door and, at sight of him, Kates
stopped the racket there.

Smiley didn't walk quite straight toward the door; he made a slight
curve that took him past my table. As he passed, he reached out and
jerked the cigar out of my hand. He stuck it in his mouth and then went
to the door and opened it.

I couldn't see in that direction, of course, and I didn't stick my head
around the corner of the el. I sat there and sweated.

"What you want? Why such a hell of a racket?" I heard Smiley
demand.

Kates' voice: "Thought Stoeger was here. That smoke——"

"Left my cigar down here," Smiley said. "Remembered it when I got
back up and came down to get it. Why all the racket?"

"It was damn near half an hour ago when I was here," Kates said
belligerently. "Cigar doesn't burn that long."

Smiley said patiently, "I couldn't sleep after you were here. I came down and got myself a drink five minutes ago. I left my cigar down here." His voice got soft, very soft. "Now get the hell out of here. You've spoiled my night already. Didn't get to sleep till two and you wake me at half-past three and come around again at four. What's the big idea, Kates?"

"You're sure Stoeger isn't——"

"I told you I'd call you if I saw him. Now, you bastard, get out of here."

I could imagine Kates turning purple. I could imagine him looking at Smiley and realizing that Smiley was half again as strong as he was.

The door slammed so hard it must have come very near to breaking the glass.

Smiley came back. Without looking back at me he said quietly, "Don't move, Doc. He might look back in a minute or two." He went on around behind the bar, got himself a glass and poured a drink. He sat down on the stool he keeps for himself back there, facing slightly to the back so his lip movement wouldn't show to anyone looking in the front window. He took a sip of the drink and a puff of my cigar.

I kept my voice as low as he'd kept his. I said, "Smiley, you ought to have your mouth washed out with soap. You told a lie."

He grinned. "Not that I know of, Doc. I told him I'd call him if I saw you. I did call him. Didn't you hear *what* I called him?"

"Smiley," I said, "this is the screwiest night I've ever been through but the screwiest thing about it is that you're developing a sense of humour. I didn't think you had it in you."

"How bad trouble are you in, Doc? What can I do?"

I said, "Nothing. Except what you just did do, and thanks to hell and back for that. It's something I've got to think out, and work out for myself, Smiley. Nobody can help me."

"Kates said, when he was here the first time, you were a ho—homi— what the hell was it?"

"Homicidal maniac," I said. "He thinks I killed two men tonight. Miles Harrison and Ralph Bonney."

"Yeah. Don't bother telling me you didn't."

I said, "Thanks, Smiley." And then it occurred to me that "Don't bother telling me you didn't" could be taken either one of two ways.

And I wondered again if I *had* been talking to myself aloud or only in my imagination while Smiley had been walking down those stairs and opening the door. I asked him, "Smiley, do you think I'm crazy?"

"I've always thought you were crazy, Doc. But crazy in a nice way."

I thought how wonderful it is to have friends. Even if I *was* crazy, there were two people in Carmel City that I could count on to go to bat for me. There was Smiley and there was Carl.

But damn it, friendship should work both ways. This was my danger and my problem and I had no business dragging Smiley into it any farther than he'd already stuck his neck. If I told Smiley that Kates had tried to kill me and still intended to, then Smiley—who hated Kates' guts already—would go out looking for Kates and like as not kill him with his bare hands, or get shot trying it. I couldn't do that to Smiley.

I said, "Smiley, finish your drink and go up to bed again. I've got to think."

"Sure there's no way I can help you, Doc?"

"Positive."

He tossed off the rest of his drink and tamped out the cigar in an ash-tray. He said, "Okay, Doc, I know you're smarter than I am, and if it's brains you need for help, I'm just in the way. Good luck to you."

He walked back to the door of the staircase. He looked carefully at the front windows to be sure nobody was looking in and then he reached inside and picked up the revolver from the step on which he'd placed it.

He came walking over to my table. He said, "Doc, if you *are* a ho— homi—what you said, you might want to kill somebody else tonight. That's loaded. I even replaced the two bullets I shot out of it earlier."

He put it down on the table in front of me, turned his back to me and went back to the stairs. I watched him go, marvelling. I'd never yet seen a man in a nightshirt who hadn't looked ridiculous. Until then. What more can a man do to prove he doesn't think you're insane than give you a loaded gun and then turn his back and walk away. And when I thought of all the times I'd razzed Smiley and ridden him, all the cracks I'd made at him, I wanted——

Well, I couldn't answer when he said "Good night, Doc," just before he closed the door behind him. Something felt a little wrong with my throat, and if I'd tried to say anything, I might have bawled.

My hand shook a little as I poured myself another drink, a short one. I was beginning to feel them and this had better be my last one, I knew.

I had to think more clearly than I'd ever thought before. I couldn't get drunk, I didn't dare.

I tried to get my mind back to what I'd been thinking about—what I'd been talking about to the little man who wasn't there—before Smiley's coming downstairs and Kates' knocking had interrupted me.

I looked across the table where Yehudi Smith, in my mind, had been sitting. But he wasn't there. I couldn't bring him back. He was dead, and he wouldn't come back.

The quiet room in the quiet night. The dim light of the single twenty-watt bulb over the cash register. The creaking of my thoughts as I tried to turn them back into the groove. Connect facts.

Lewis Carroll and bloody murder.

Through the Looking-Glass and What Alice Found There.

What *had* Alice found there?

Chessmen, and a game of chess. And Alice herself had been a pawn. That was why, of course, she'd crossed the third square by railroad. With the smoke alone worth a thousand pounds a puff—almost as expensive as the smoke from my cigar might have been had not Smiley taken it out of my hand and claimed it as his own.

Chessmen, and a game of chess.

But who was the *player*?

And suddenly I knew. Illogically, because he didn't have a shadow of a motive. The Why I did not see, but Yehudi Smith had told me the How, and now I saw the Who.

The pattern. Whoever had arranged tonight's little chess problem played chess all right, and played it well. Looking-glass chess and real chess, both. And he knew me well—which meant I knew him, too. He knew my weaknesses, the things I'd fall for. He *knew* I'd go with Yehudi Smith on the strength of that mad, weird story Smith had told me.

But *why?* What had he to gain? He'd killed Miles Harrison, Ralph Bonney and Yehudi Smith. And he'd left the money Miles and Ralph had been carrying in that brief-case and put it in the back of my car, with the two bodies.

Then money hadn't been the motive. Either that, or the motive had been money in such large quantity that the couple of thousand dollars Bonney had been carrying didn't matter.

But wasn't a man concerned who was one of the richest men in Carmel City? Ralph Bonney. His fireworks factory, his other investments, his real estate must have added up to—well, maybe half a million dollars. A man shooting for half a million dollars can well abandon the proceeds of a two-thousand dollar holdup and leave them with the bodies of the men he has killed, to help pin the crime on the pawn he has selected, to divert suspicion from himself.

Connect facts.

Ralph Bonney was divorced today. He was murdered tonight.

Then Miles Harrison's death was incidental. Yehudi Smith had been another pawn.

A warped mind, but a brilliant mind. A cold, cruel mind. And yet, paradoxically, a mind that loved fantasy, as I did, that loved Lewis Carroll, as I did.

I started to pour myself another drink and then remembered that I still had only part of the answer, and that even if I had it all, I hadn't the slightest idea what I could do with it, without a shred of evidence, or an iota of proof.

Without even an idea, in my own mind, of the reason, the motive. But there must be one; the rest of it was too well planned, too logical.

There was one possibility that I could see.

I sat there listening a while to be sure there was no car approaching; the night was so quiet that I could have heard one at least a block away.

I looked at the gun Smiley had given me back, hesitated, and finally put it in my pocket. Then I went into the back room and let myself out of the window into the dark alley.

Carl Trenholm's house was three blocks away. Luckily, it was on the street next to Oak Street and parallel to it. I could make all of the distance through the alley except for the streets I'd have to cross.

I heard a car coming as I approached the second street and I ducked down and hid behind a garbage can until it had gone by. It was going slowly and it was probably either Hank and the sheriff or the two deputies. I didn't look out to see for fear they might flash a spotlight down the alley.

I waited until the sound of it died away completely before I crossed the street.

I let myself in the back gate of Carl's place. With his wife away, I wasn't positive which bedroom he'd be sleeping in, but I found pebbles and tossed them at the most likely window and it was the right one.

It went up and Carl's head came out. I stepped close to the house so I wouldn't have to yell. I said, "It's Doc, Carl. Don't light a light anywhere in the house. But come down to the back door."

"Coming, Doc." He closed the window. I went up on the back porch and waited until the door opened and I went in. I closed the door behind me and the kitchen was as black as the inside of a tomb.

Carl said, "Damned if I know where a flashlight is, Doc. Can't we put on a light? I feel like hell."

"No, leave it off," I told him. I struck a match, though, to find my way to a chair and it showed me Carl in rumpled pyjamas, his hair mussed and looking like he was in for the grandfather of all hangovers.

He sat down, too, while the match flared. "What's it about, Doc? Kates and Ganzer were here looking for you. Waked me up a while ago, but they didn't tell me much. Are you in a jam, Doc? *Did* you kill somebody?"

"No," I said. "Listen, you're Ralph Bonney's lawyer, aren't you? I mean on everything, not just the divorce today."

"Yes."

"Who's his heir, now that he's divorced?"

"Doc, I'm afraid I can't tell you that. A lawyer isn't supposed to tell his clients' business. You know that as well as I do."

"Didn't Kates tell you Ralph Bonney is dead, Carl? And Miles Harrison? They were murdered on their way back from Neilsville with the payroll, somewhere around midnight."

"My God," Carl said. "No, Kates didn't tell me."

I said, "I know you're still not supposed to tell his business until a will is probated, if there is one. But listen, let me make a guess and you can tell me if I'm wrong. If I guess right, you won't have to confirm it; just keep your mouth shut."

"Go ahead, Doc."

"Bonney had an illegitimate son about twenty-three years ago. But he supported the boy's mother all her life until she died recently; she worked, too, as a milliner but he gave her enough extra so that she lived better than she would have otherwise, and she sent the boy to college and gave him every break."

I stopped there and waited and Carl didn't say anything.

I went on, "Bonney still gave the boy an allowance. That's how he— hell, let's call him by name—that's how Al Grainger has been living without working. And unless he knows he's in Bonney's will, he's got proof of his parentage and can claim the bulk of the estate anyway. And it must be half a million."

Carl said, "I'll talk. It'll run about three hundred thousand. And you guessed right on Al Grainger, but how you guessed it, I don't know. Bonney's relations to Mrs. Grainger and to Al have been the best-kept secret I've ever known of. In fact, outside the parties concerned, I was the only person who ever knew—or even suspected. How did you guess?"

"By what happened to me tonight—and that's too complicated to explain right now. But Al plays chess and has the type of mind to do things the complicated way, and that's the way they happened. And he knows Lewis Carroll and——" I stopped because I was still after facts and I didn't want to start explaining.

The night was almost over. I saw a greenish gleam in the darkness that reminded me Carl wore a wrist watch with a luminous dial. "What time is it?" I asked him.

The gleam vanished as he turned the dial toward himself. "Almost five o'clock. About ten minutes off. Listen Doc, you've got so much you might as well have the rest. Yes, Al has proof of his parentage. And, as an only child, illegitimate or not, he can claim the entire estate now that Bonney isn't married. He could have cut in for a fraction of it, of course, even before the divorce."

"Didn't he leave a will?"

"Ralph didn't ever make a will. Superstitious about it. I've often tried to talk him into making one, but he never would."

"And Al Grainger knew that?"

Carl said, "I imagine he would have."

"Is there any reason why Al would have been in such a hurry?" I asked. "I mean, would there have been any change in status if he'd waited a while instead of killing Bonney the night after the divorce?"

Carl thought a minute. "Bonney was planning to leave tomorrow for a long vacation. Al would have had to wait several months, and maybe he figured Bonney might re-marry—meet someone on the cruise he was going to take. It happens that way, sometimes, on the rebound after a divorce. And Bonney is—was only fifty-two."

I nodded—to myself, since Carl couldn't see me in the darkness. That last bit of information covered everything on the motive end.

I knew everything now, except the details and they didn't matter much. I knew why Al had done everything that he had done; he had to make an airtight frame on someone because once he claimed Bonney's estate, his own motive would be obvious. I could even guess some of the reasons why he'd picked me for the scapegoat.

He must have hated me, and kept it carefully under cover. I could see a reason for it, now that I knew more about him. I've got a loose tongue and often swear at people affectionately, if you know what I mean. How often, when Al had beaten me in a game of chess had I grinned at him and said, "All right, you bastard. But try to do it again."

Never dreaming, of course, that he *was* one, and knew it.

He must have hated me like hell. In some ways he could have picked an easier victim, someone more likely than I to have committed murder and robbery for money. Choosing me, his plan took more gobbledegook; he had to give me such a mad story to tell that nobody would believe a word of it and would think, instead, that I'd gone insane. Of course, too, he knew how much Kates hated me; he counted on that.

A sudden thought shook me; could Kates have been in on the deal with Al? That would account for his trying to kill me rather than lock me up. Maybe that was the deal—for a twenty or fifty thousand dollar cut of the estate, Kates had agreed to shoot me down under the pretence that I had attacked him or had tried to escape.

No, I decided on second thought, it hadn't been that way. I'd been alone with Kates in his office for almost half an hour while Hank Ganzer had been on his way back from Neilsville. It would have been too easy for Kates to have killed me then, planted a weapon on me and claimed that I'd come in and attacked him. And when the two bodies had been found in my car, the story would have been perfectly credible. It would even have pointed up the indication that I'd gone homicidally insane.

No, Kates' motives for wanting to kill me had been personal, sheer malice because of the things I'd written about him in editorials and the way I'd fought him in elections. He'd wanted to kill me and had seen a sudden opportunity when the bodies had been found in my car. He'd passed up a much better chance because, when I was alone with him for so long in his office, he hadn't known the bodies were there.

No, definitely this was a one-man job, except for Yehudi Smith. Al had hired Smith to keep me diverted, but when Smith's job was done, he was eliminated. Another pawn. Chess isn't a team game.

Carl said, "How are *you* mixed in this, Doc? What can I do?"

"Nothing," I said. It was my problem, not Carl's. I'd kept Smiley out of it; I'd keep Carl out of it, too. Except for the information and help he'd already given me. "Go up to bed, Carl. I've got a little more thinking to do."

"Hell with that. I can't sleep with you sitting down here thinking. But I'll sit here and shut up unless you talk to me. You can't tell whether I'm here or not anyway, if I shut up."

I said, "Shut up, then."

Proof, I thought. But what proof? Somewhere, but God knew where, was the dead body of the actor Al had hired to play the role of Yehudi. But this had been planned, and well planned. Suitable disposal of that body had been arranged for long before Al had taken it away from the Wentworth place. It wasn't going to turn up at random and one guess was as good as another as to where he'd hidden or buried it. He'd had hours to do it in and he'd known in advance every step he was going to take.

The car in which Yehudi Smith had driven me to the Wentworth house and which he'd switched for my own car after he'd used mine for the supposed holdup. No, I couldn't find that car as proof and it wouldn't mean anything if I did. It could have been—probably was—a stolen car, and now returned to wherever he'd stolen it from, never missed by its owner. And I didn't even remember what make or model it was. All I remember was that it had an onyx gear shift knob and a push-button radio. I didn't even know whether it was a Cadillac, convertible or a Ford business coupé.

Had Al arranged any kind of an alibi for himself?

Maybe, maybe not, but what did it matter unless I could find something against him besides motive? That, and my own certainty that he'd done it. I hadn't any alibi, none at all. I had an incredible story and two bodies and the stolen money in my car. And a sheriff and three deputies looking for me and ready to shoot on sight.

I had the murder weapon in my pocket. And another gun, too, a loaded one.

Could I go to Al Grainger and scare him into writing out and signing a confession?

He'd laugh at me. I'd laugh at myself for trying. A man with the warped brain that would work out something like Al's plan tonight wasn't going to tell me what time it was just because I pointed a gun at him.

A faint touch of light was showing at the windows. I could even make out Carl sitting there across the table from me.

"Carl," I said.

"Yes. Doc? Say, I was letting you think, but I'm glad you spoke. Just had an idea."

"An idea's what I need," I told him. "What is it?"

"Want a drink?"

I asked, "Is that the idea?"

"That's the idea. Look, I'm hung over to hell and back and I can't have one with you, but I just realized what a lousy host I was. Do you want one?"

"Thanks," I said, "but I had a drink. Listen, Carl, talk to me about Al Grainger. Don't ask me what to say. Just talk."

"Anything, at random?"

"Anything, at random."

"Well, he's always impressed me as being a little off the beam. Brilliant, but—well, twisted, somehow. Maybe his knowledge of who and what he was contributed to that. Smiley always felt that, too; he's mentioned it to me. Not that Smiley knows who or what Al is, but he just felt something was wrong."

I said, "My opinion of Smiley has changed a lot tonight. He's smarter, and a better guy, than both of us put together, Carl. But go on about Al."

"Touch of Oedipus, complicated by bastardy. Probably, in some obscure way, managed to blame Bonney for his mother's death. Not a real paranoiac, but near enough to do something like that. Sadism—most of us have a touch of it, but Al a little more than most."

I said, "Most of us have a touch of everything. Go on."

"Pyrophobia. But you know about that. Not that we haven't all got phobias. Your acrophobia and my being afraid of cats. But Al's is pretty bad. So afraid of fire that he doesn't smoke and I've noticed him wince when I've lighted a cig——"

"Shut up, Carl," I said.

I should have thought of it myself, sooner. A lot sooner.

I said, "I'll have that drink, Carl. Just one, but a good one."

I didn't need it physically, but I needed it mentally this time. I was scared stiff at the very thought of what I was going to do.

CHAPTER FIFTEEN

One, two! One, two! and through and through
The vorpal blade went snicker-snack!
He left it dead, and with its head
He went galumphing back.

THE windows were faint grey rectangles; now with my eyes accustomed to the decreasing darkness, I could see Carl almost clearly as he went to the cupboard and groped until he had the bottle he was looking for.

He said, "Doc, you sound happy enough that I'll have one with you. Hair of the dog, for me. Kill or cure."

He got two glasses, too, from over the sink, breaking only one glass by knocking it into the sink in the process. He said a nasty word and then brought the glasses to the table. I struck a match and held it while he poured whisky into them.

He said, "Damn you, Doc, if you're going to do this often, I'm going to get some luminous paint. I could paint bands around the glasses and the bottle. And say, know what else I could do? I could paint a chessboard and a set of chessmen with luminous paint, too. Then we could sit here and play chess in the dark."

"I'm playing, Carl, right now. I just reached the seventh square. Maybe somebody'll crown me on the next move, when I reach the king-row. Have you got any cleaning fluid?"

He started to reach for his glass, but he pulled his hand back and looked at me instead.

"Cleaning fluid? Isn't whisky good enough for you?"

"I don't want it to drink," I explained. "I want it not to burn."

He shook his head a trifle. "Again and slowly."

"I want some of the kind that isn't inflammable. You know what I mean."

"Wife's got some kind of cleaning fluid around. Whether it's that kind or not, I don't know. I'll look."

He looked, using my matches and examining the labels of a row of bottles in the compartment under the sink. He came up with one and looked at it closely. "Nope. This is marked 'Danger' in big letters and "Keep away from fire.' Guess we haven't got the non-inflammable kind."

I sighed. It would have been simple if Carl had had the right brand. I had some myself, at home, but I didn't want to go there. It meant a trip to the supermarket.

And I didn't ask Carl for a candle. I could get that at the supermarket, too, and I neither wanted Carl to think I was crazy or to have to explain to him what I was going to do.

We had our drink. Carl shuddered at his, but got it down. He said, "Doc, listen, isn't there *anything* I can do?"

I turned back at the door. "You've done plenty." I told him. "But if you want to do more, you might get dressed and ready. I might be phoning you soon if everything goes all right. I might need you then."

"Doc, wait. I'll get dressed now, and——"

"You'd be in the way, Carl," I told him.

And got out quickly before he could press me any farther. If he'd even guessed how bad a jam I was in or what a damn fool thing I was going to do, he'd have knocked me down and tied me up before he'd have let me out of there.

Dim grey light of early morning now, and I no longer had to grope my way. I'd forgotten to ask Carl the time again, but it must be about a quarter after five.

I was under greater risk, now, of being seen if Kates and the deputies were still cruising around looking for me, but I had a hunch that they'd have given up by now, convinced that I'd holed in somewhere. Probably now they were concentrating on the roads so I couldn't get out of town. And getting out of town was the farthest thing from my mind.

I stayed in the alleys, just the same. Back the way I'd come and ready to dive between garages or behind a garbage can at the first sound of a car. But there weren't any cars; five-fifteen is early even in Carmel City.

The supermarket wasn't open yet. I wrapped my handkerchief around the butt of one of my two revolvers—Two-Gun Stoeger, they call me—and broke a pane in one of the back windows. It made a hell of a racket, but there aren't any residences in that block and nobody heard me, or at least nobody did anything about it.

I let myself in and started my shopping.

Cleaning fluid. Two kinds; I needed some of the non-inflammable kind and, now that I thought of it, a bottle of the kind that was marked "Danger. Keep away from fire."

I opened both of them and they smelled about alike. I poured the inflammable kind down the drain of the sink at the back and replaced it with the kind that doesn't burn.

I even made sure that it wouldn't burn; I poured some on a rag and tried to light the rag. Maybe it would have been in keeping with everything else that had been happening if that rag *had* burned and I hadn't been able to put it out, if I'd burned the supermarket down and added arson to my other accomplishments of the night. But the rag wouldn't burn any more than if I'd soaked it with water instead of the gasoline-smelling cleaning fluid.

I thought out carefully what other items I'd need, and shopped for them; some rolls of one-inch adhesive tape, a candle, and a cake of soap. I'd heard that a cake of soap, inside a sock, made a good blackjack; the soap is soft enough to stun without killing. I took off one of my socks and made myself a blackjack.

My pockets were pretty well laden by the time I left the supermarket—by the same window through which I'd entered. I was pretty far gone in crime by them; it never occurred to me to leave money for my purchases.

It was almost daylight. A clear grey dawn that looked like the herald of a good day—for someone; whether for me or not I'd know soon.

I stuck to the alleys, back the way I'd come and three blocks on past Carl's house.

Al Grainger's. A one-storey, three-room house, about the size of mine.

It was almost six o'clock by then. He was asleep by now, if he was ever going to sleep. And somehow I thought he *would* be asleep by now. He'd have been through with everything he had to do by two o'clock, four hours ago. What he'd done might have kept him awake for a while, but not into the next day.

I cased the joint, and sighed with relief at one problem solved when I saw that the bedroom window wasn't closed. It opened on to the back porch and I could step into it easily.

I bent and stepped through it. I didn't make much noise and Al Grainger, sleeping soundly in the bed, didn't awaken. I had my gun—the loaded one—in my right hand and ready to use in case he did.

But I kept my right hand and the loaded gun out of sight. I got the rusty, unloaded Iver-Johnson, the gun that had been used as a bludgeon to kill Miles and Bonney, into my left hand. I had a test in mind which, if it worked, would be absolute proof to me that Al was guilty. If it didn't work, it wouldn't disprove it and I'd go ahead just the same, but it didn't cost anything to try.

It was still dim in the room and I reached out with my left hand and turned on the lamp that stood beside the bed. I wanted him to see that gun. He moved restlessly as the light went on, but he didn't awaken.

"Al," I said.

He wakened then, all right. He sat up in bed and stared at me. I said, "Put up your hands, Al," and held the gun in my left hand pointed at him, standing far enough back that he couldn't grab at me, but near enough that he could see the gun clearly in the pale glow of the lamp I'd lighted.

He looked from my face to the gun and back again. He threw back the sheet to get out of bed. He said, "Don't be a fool, Doc. That gun isn't loaded and it wouldn't shoot if it was."

If I needed any more proof, I had it.

He was starting to move his feet toward the edge of the bed when I brought my right hand, holding the other gun, around into sight. I said, "This one is loaded, and works."

155

He stopped moving his feet. I dropped the rusty gun into my coat pocket. I said, "Turn around Al."

He hesitated and I cocked the revolver. It was aimed at him from about five feet, too close to miss him if I pulled the trigger and just too far for him to risk grabbing at, especially from an awkward sitting-up-in-bed position. I could see him considering the odds, coldly, impartially.

He decided they weren't good. And he decided, probably, that if he let me take him, it wouldn't matter to his plans anyway. If I turned him over to the police along with my story, it wouldn't strengthen my story in the least.

"Turn around, Al," I repeated.

He still stared at me calculatingly. I could see what he was thinking; if he turned, I was probably going to slug him with the butt of the revolver and whatever my intentions, I might hit too hard. And if I killed him, even accidentally, it wouldn't help him any to know that they'd got me for one extra murder. I repeated, "Turn around, and put your hands out in back of you."

I could see some of the tenseness go out of him at that. If I was only going to tie him up——

He turned around. I quickly switched the revolver to my left hand and pulled out the improvised blackjack I'd made of a sock and a cake of soap. I made a silent prayer that I'd guess right on the swing and not hit too hard or not hard enough, and I swung.

The thud scared me. I thought I'd killed him, and I knew that he wasn't shamming when he dropped back flat on the bed because his head hit the head of the bed with a second thud that was almost as loud as the first.

And if he had been shamming he could have taken me easily, because I was so scared that I put the revolver down. I couldn't even put it in my pocket because it was cocked and I didn't know how to uncock it without shooting it off. So I put it on the night stand beside the bed and bent over him to feel his heart. It was still beating.

I got the rolls of adhesive tape out of my pocket and started to work. I taped around his mouth so he couldn't yell, and I taped his legs together at the ankles and at the knees. I taped his left wrist to his left thigh, and I used a whole roll of adhesive to tape his right arm against his side above the elbow. His right hand had to be free.

I found some clothes-line in the kitchen and tied him to the bed, managing as I did so to pull him up into an almost sitting position against the head of the bed.

I got a pad of paper, foolscap, from his desk and I put it and my ball-point pen within reach of his right hand.

There wasn't anything I could do but sit down and wait, then.

Ten minutes, maybe fifteen, and it was getting pretty light outside. I began to get impatient. Probably there wasn't any hurry; Al Grainger always slept late so no one would miss him for a long time yet, but the waiting was horrible.

I decided that I could take a drink again and that I needed one. I went out into his kitchen and hunted till I found a bottle. It was gin instead of whisky, but it would serve the purpose. It tasted horrible.

When I got back to the bedroom he was awake. So wide awake that I felt pretty sure that he'd been playing possum for a while, stalling for time. He was trying desperately with his free right hand to peel off the tape that held his left wrist to his thigh.

But with his right arm held tight against his side at the elbow he wasn't making much headway. When I picked up the gun off the night stand he stopped trying. He glared at me.

I said, "Hi, Al. We're in the seventh square."

I wasn't in any hurry now, none at all. I sat down comfortably before I went on.

"Listen, Al," I told him, "I left your right hand free so you can use that paper and the pen. I want you to do a little writing for me. I'll hold the pad for you so you can see what you're writing. Or don't you feel in the mood to write, Al?"

He merely lay back quietly and closed his eyes.

I said, "All I want you to write is that you killed Ralph Bonney and Miles Harrison last night. That you took my car out and intercepted them on the way back from Neilsville, probably on foot with my car out of sight. They knew you and would stop for you and let you in the car. So you got in the back seat and before Miles, who'd be driving, could start the car again you slugged him over the head and then slugged Bonney.

157

Then you put their bodies in my car and left theirs somewhere off the road. And then you drove to the Wentworth place and left my car instead of whatever car I'd been driven there in. Or am I wrong on any little details, Al?"

He didn't answer, not that I'd expected him to.

I said, "There'll be quite a bit of writing, because I want you also to explain how you hired an actor to use the name of Yehudi Smith and give me such an incredible story to tell that no one would ever believe me. I want you to tell how you had him entice me to the Wentworth place—and about that bottle you left there and what was in it. And that you'd instructed him that he was to drink it. And what his right name was and what you did with his body."

I said, "I guess that'll be enough for you to write, Al. You needn't write what the motive was; that'll be obvious after your relationship to Ralph Bonney comes to light, as it will. And you needn't write all the little details about how or when you let the air out of my tyres so I wouldn't be using my car nor how or when you used my shop to print that card with the name Yehudi Smith and my union label number. And you needn't write why you picked me to take the blame for the murders. In fact, I'm not proud of that part of it at all. It makes me a little ashamed of the thing I'm going to have to do in order to persuade you to do the writing I've been talking about."

I *was* a little ashamed, but not enough so to keep me from doing it.

I took the bottle of non-inflammable cleaning fluid that smelled like gasoline and opened it.

Al Grainger's eyes opened, too, as I began to sprinkle it over the sheets and his pyjamas. I managed to hold the bottle so he could read the "Danger" warning and, if his eyes were good enough for the smaller type, the "Keep away from fire" part.

I emptied the whole bottle, ending up with quite a big wet spot of it at a point at one side of his knees where he could see it clearly. The room reeked with the gasoline-like odour.

I got out the candle and my knife and cut a piece an inch long off the top of the candle. I smoothed out the wet spot on the sheet and put the candle top down carefully.

158

"I'm going to light this, Al, and you'd better not move much or you'll knock it over. And I'm sure a pyrophobiac wouldn't like what would happen to him then. And you're a pyrophobiac, Al."

His eyes were wide with horror as I lighted the match. If his mouth hadn't been taped, he'd have screamed in terror. Every muscle of his body was rigid.

He tried to play possum on me, again, probably figuring I wouldn't go through with it if he was unconscious, if I thought he'd fainted. He could do it with his eyes, but the muscles of the rest of his body gave him away. He couldn't relax them if it would have saved his life.

I lighted the candle, and sat down again.

"An inch of candle, Al," I said. "Maybe ten minutes if you stay as still as that. Sooner if you get reckless and wriggle a toe or finger. That candle isn't too stable standing there on a soft mattress."

His eyes were open again, staring at that candle burning down toward the soaked sheet, staring in utter horror. I hated myself for what I was doing to him, but I kept on doing it just the same. I thought of three men murdered tonight and steeled myself. And after all, Al's only danger was in his mind. That wet spot on the sheet was stuff that would keep the sheet itself from burning.

"Ready to write, Al?"

His horror-filled eyes shifted from the candle to my face, but he didn't nod; I thought for a moment that he was calling my bluff, and then I realized that the reason he didn't nod was because he was afraid to make even the slight muscular movement for fear of knocking over the short candle.

I said, "All right, Al. I'll see if you're ready. If you aren't, I'll put the candle back where it was, and I'll let it keep burning meanwhile so you won't have gained any time." I picked up the candle gently and put it down on the night stand.

I held the pad. He started to write and then stopped, and I reached for the candle. The pen started moving again.

After a while I said, "That's enough. Just sign it."

I sighed with relief and went over to the telephone. Carl Trenholm must have been sitting beside his own phone; he answered almost before it had finished ringing the first time.

"Dressed and ready?" I asked him.

"Right, Doc. What do I do?"

"I've got Al Grainger's confession. I want it turned over to the law to clear me, but it's not safe for me to do it direct. Kates would shoot before he'd read and some of the deputies might. You'll have to do it for me, Carl."

"Where are you? at Al's?"

"Yes."

"I'll be around. And I'll bring Ganzer to get Al. It's all right; Hank won't shoot. I've been talking reason to him and he admits somebody else could have put those bodies in your car. And when I tell him there's a confession from Grainger, he'll listen."

"How about Kates, though? And how come you were talking to Hank Ganzer?"

"He called up here, looking for Kates. Kates left him to go back to the office an hour or two ago and never got to the office and they don't know where he is. But don't worry, Kates won't take any shots at you if you're with Ganzer and me both. I'll be right around."

I phoned Pete and told him that all hell had been popping and that now we had a story we could use, one even bigger than the ones that had got away. He said he'd get right down to the shop and get the fire going under the Linotype's metal pot. "I was just leaving anyway, Doc," he said. "It's half-past seven."

It was. I looked out the window and saw that it was broad daylight. I sat down and jittered until Carl and Hank got there.

It was eight o'clock exactly when I got to the office. Once Hank had seen that confession he'd let Carl and me talk him into letting Grainger do any explaining that remained so I could get the paper out in time. It was going to take me a good two hours to get that story written and we'd probably go to press a little later than usual, anyway.

Pete got to work dismantling page one to make room for it—and plenty of room. I phoned the restaurant and talked them into sending up a big thermos jug of hot, black coffee and started pounding my typewriter.

The phone rang and I picked it up. "Doc Stoeger?" it said. "This is Dr. Buchan at the asylum. You were so kind last night about not running the story about Mrs. Griswald's escape and recapture that I decided it was only fair to tell you that you can run it after all, if there's still time."

"There's still time," I said. "We're going to be late going to press anyway. And thanks. But what came up? I thought Mrs. G. didn't want to worry her daughter in Springfield."

"Her daughter knows anyway. A friend of hers here—one whom we went to see while we were hunting our patient—phoned her to tell her about it. And she telephoned the asylum to be sure her mother was all right. So she already knows and you might as well have the story after all."

I said, "Fine, Dr. Buchan. Thanks a lot for calling."

Back to the typewriter. The black coffee came and I drank almost a full cup of it the first gulp and damn near scalded myself.

The asylum story was quick and easy to get out of the way so I wrote it up first. I'd just finished when the phone rang again.

"Mr. Stoeger?" it asked me. "This is Ward Howard, superintendent of the fireworks factory. We had a slight accident in the plant yesterday that I'd like you to run a short story on, if it's not too late."

"It's not too late," I said, "provided the accident was in the Roman candle department. Was it?"

"Oh, so you already knew. Do you have the details or shall I give them to you?"

I let him give them and took notes and then I asked him how come they *wanted* the story printed.

"Change of policy, Mr. Stoeger. You see there have been rumours going around town about accidents here that don't happen—but are supposed to have happened and to have been kept out of the paper. I'm afraid my grammar's a bit involved there. I mean that we've decided that if the truth is printed about accidents that really do happen, it will help prevent false rumours and wild stories."

I told him I understood and thanked him.

I drank more black coffee and worked a while on the Bonney-Harrison-Smith murder story and then sandwiched in the Roman candle department story and then went back to the big story.

All I needed now was——

Captain Evans of the state police came in. I glared up at him and he grinned down at me.

I said, "Don't tell me. You've come to tell me that I can, after all, run the story of Smiley's and my little ride with the two gangsters and how Smiley captured one and killed one. It's just what I need. I can spare a stick of type back in the want ads."

He grinned again and pulled up a chair. He sat down in it, but I paid no further attention; I went on typing.

Then he pushed his hat back on his head and said quietly, "That's right, Doc."

I made four typing errors in a three-letter word and then turned around and looked at him. "Huh?" I said. "I was kidding. Wasn't I?"

"Maybe you were, but I'm not. You can run the story, Doc. They got Gene Kelley in Chicago two hours ago."

I groaned happily. Then I glared at him again. I said, "Then get the hell out of here. I've got to work."

"Don't you want the rest of the story?"

"What rest of it? I don't need details of how they got Kelley, just so they got him. That's, from my point of view, a footnote on the local angle, and the local angle is what happened *here* in the county to George and Bat—and to Smiley and me. Now scram."

I typed another sentence. He said, "Doc," and the way he said it made me take my hands away from the typewriter and look at him.

He said, "Doc, relax. It *is* local. There was one thing I didn't tell you last night because it was *too* local and too hot. One other thing we got out of Bat Masters. They weren't heading for Chicago or Gary right away. They were going to hole up overnight at a hideout for crooks—it's a farm run by a man named George Dixon, up in the hills. An isolated place. We knew Dixon as an ex-crook but never guessed he was running a rest home for boys who were hiding out from the law. We raided it last night. We got four criminals wanted in Chicago who were staying there. And we found, among other things, some letters and papers that told us where Gene Kelley was staying. We phoned Chicago quick and they got him, so you can run the whole story—the other members of the gang won't keep that hotel date anyway. But we'll settle for having Kelley in the bag—and the rest of our haul at the Dixon farm. And that's local, Doc. Want names and such?"

162

I wanted names and such. I grabbed a pencil. Where I was going to *put* the story, I didn't know. Evans talked a while and I took notes until I had all I wanted and then I said again, "Now *please* don't give me any more. I'm going nuts already."

He laughed and got up. He said, "Okay, Doc." He strolled to the door and then turned around after he was half-way through it. "Then you don't want to know about Sheriff Kates being under arrest."

He went on through and was half-way down the stairs before I caught him and dragged him back.

Dixon, who ran the crook hideout, had been paying protection to Kates and had proof of it. When he'd been raided he'd thought Kates had double-crossed him, and he talked. The state police had headed for Kates' office and had picked him up as he was entering the courthouse at six o'clock.

I sent out for more black coffee.

There was only one more interruption and it came just before we were finally closing the forms at half-past eleven.

Clyde Andrews. He said, "Doc, I want to thank you again for what you did last night. And to tell you that the boy and I have had a long talk and everything is going to be all right."

"That's wonderful, Clyde."

"Another thing, Doc, and I hope this isn't bad news for you. I mean, I hope you were deciding not to sell the paper, because I got a telegram from my brother in Ohio; he's definitely taking that offer from out West, so the deal on the paper is off. I'm sorry if you were going to decide to sell."

I said, "That's wonderful, Clyde. But hold the line a second. I'm going to put an ad in the paper to sell it instead."

I yelled across the room to Pete, "Hey, Pete, kill something somewhere and set up an ad in sixty-point type. 'For Sale, The Carmel City Clarion, Price, One Million Dollars.' "

Back into the phone, "Hear that, Clyde?"

He chuckled. "I'm glad you feel that way about it, Doc. Listen there's one more thing. Mr. Rogers just called me. He says that we've discovered that the Scouts are going to use the church gym next Tuesday instead of this Tuesday. So we're going to have the rummage sale after all. If you haven't gone to press and if you haven't got enough news to fill out——"

I nearly choked, but I managed to tell him we'd run the story.

I got to Smiley's at half-past twelve with the first paper off the press in my hands. Held carefully.

I put it proudly on the bar. "Read," I told Smiley. "But first the bottle and a glass. I'm half dead and I haven't had a drink for almost six hours. I'm too keyed up to sleep. And I need three quick ones."

I had three quick ones while Smiley read the headlines.

The room began to waver a little and I realized I'd better get sober and quickly. I said, "Good night, Smiley. 'Sbeen wonnerful knowing you. I gotta——"

I started for the door.

Smiley said, "Doc. Let me drive you home." His voice came from miles and miles away. I saw him start around the end of the bar.

"Doc," he was saying, "sit down and hang on till I get there before you fall down flat on your face."

But the nearest stool was miles away through the brillig, and slithy toves were gimbling at me from the wabe. Smiley's warning had been at least half a second too late.